PRAISE FOR POLLY DUGAN'S
The House of Cavanaugh

"*The House of Cavanaugh* is a moving, elegantly told novel about life and death, about familial love and familial secrets, and about how the past persists in the present, no matter how much we'd like to think otherwise. Polly Dugan is a wise and sensitive writer, and with this beautiful novel she'll break your heart."

—Edan Lepucki, *NYT* bestselling author of *Time's Mouth* and *California*

★ ★ ★

"*The House of Cavanaugh* is a brilliant, gripping novel built around the secrets we keep from the world, and the ones we keep from ourselves. Polly Dugan writes like a dream. Her sentences are piercing and true. This book takes clean aim at the messy truths of the human heart. I couldn't put it down."

—Steve Almond, author of *All the Secrets of the World* and *Truth Is the Arrow, Mercy Is the Bow*

★ ★ ★

"Polly Dugan writes about the complexities of family and marriage, love and loss, with authenticity and deep compassion. This artfully layered novel succeeds at being both a compelling page-turner and a sensitive, nuanced portrait of real people living real lives. I devoured it with eagerness and admiration."

—Elise Juska, author of *Reunion*

★ ★ ★

"A family confronts a long-buried secret in Dugan's novel. A well-paced...generational drama that holds the reader's interest as the decades progress."

—*Kirkus Reviews*

★ ★ ★

"I was caught up in this rich, engrossing family saga from the first page to the last, wondering how withheld secrets would transform these relatable characters' lives. The story unfolds naturally and is told with great empathy for all; no one is a villain, no one a true deceiver. The Cavanaughs are simply alive, and as flawed and immutably human as the rest of us."

—Laura Sims, author of *Looker* and *How Can I Help You*

★ ★ ★

"*The House of Cavanaugh* is a knockout. One of the most emotionally astute books I've read in years. How many complex relationships can be explored in one short novel? I think Polly Dugan redefines the answer."

—Susan Perabo, author of *The Fall of Lisa Bellow*

★ ★ ★

"What a thrill to read Polly Dugan's gorgeous new novel about a long-held secret that ruptures and binds two families over decades. There's so much to admire about *The House of Cavanaugh*: the depth and complexity of characterization, the fluid movement between perspectives and over time, the surprising revelations. In the end, what makes the book so moving to me is that despite the range of painful emotions it explores—grief, betrayal, resentment—what wins out above all else is love, which remains when everything else fades away."

—Scott Nadelson, author of *Trust Me*

"I have been a fan of Polly Dugan's writing since I read *So Much a Part of You*—she is a master at peeling back the layers of complex interpersonal dynamics and cutting to the emotional core of the things we hide and hold onto. I was so happy to see a family from that collection come back to fill the pages of *The House of Cavanaugh*, so that I could take a deeper dive into the relationships that Polly untangles - years of secrets and the subsequent revelations - and again I am held in the raw honesty and sharp truth of a beautiful storyteller. This novel will live with me for a very long time."

—Jodi Angel, author of *Biggest Little Girl* and *You Only Get Letters from Jail*

★ ★ ★

"*The House of Cavanaugh* is a beautifully wrought portrait of the ways hidden truths carve pathways through generations. Elegantly written and deeply moving, it considers the quiet devastations caused by secrets kept and the redemptive power of truths finally told. A poignant and fearless exploration of love, loss, and the complexities of family."

—Emily Raymond, *NYT* bestselling coauthor of *First Love*

★ ★ ★

"I love family sagas and *The House of Cavanaugh* hits all the right notes. Polly Dugan has again proven to be an excellent architect of family stories, written with love, humility, and wisdom. This wonderful novel will bring tears to your eyes and make you laugh out loud, and you will not easily or quickly forget this book or these characters. Truly a treasure, a fabulous read."

—Laura L. Engel, author of *You'll Forget This Ever Happened – Secrets, Shame and Adoption in the 1960s*

The
HOUSE
of
CAVANAUGH

A Novel

POLLY DUGAN

Sibylline Press

Sibylline Press

Copyright © 2025 by Polly Dugan

All Rights Reserved. Published in the United States by Sibylline Press, an imprint of All Things Book LLC, California. Sibylline Press is dedicated to publishing the brilliant work of women authors ages 50 and older.

www.sibyllinepress.com

Distributed to the trade by Publishers Group West
ISBN Trade: 9781960573469
eBook ISBN: 9781960573520

Library of Congress Control Number: 2025932910

Cover Design: Alicia Feltman
Book Production: Aaron Laughlin

This book is a work of fiction. Names, characters, places, and incidents are either a product of the author's imagination or are used fictitiously. Any resemblance to actual persons, living or dead, is entirely coincidental.

HUMAN AUTHORED: Any use of this publication to train artificial intelligence (AI) technologies to generate text is expressly prohibited.

For Finn and Brady, my treasures

The HOUSE of CAVANAUGH

A Novel

POLLY DUGAN

NEW YORK

1989

1

God help me, this dying is lonely fucking business. And at forty-eight I'm not old enough for it.

But I am old enough to know none of us can avoid life's isolating milestones—both the celebrations and the heartbreaks. Brides and grooms, laboring mothers and expectant fathers, divorced and surviving spouses, estranged siblings, inconsolable parents and bereft children have all known the staggering isolation I'm feeling. For some, it's more acute or lasts longer than it does for others. And yet I could look in any direction and handily find at least ten people who have survived or are surviving any one of those life events and could counsel someone who needs to hear their story of resilience. *I was afraid I wouldn't get through it, but I did. You will, too. Everything's going to be okay.*

But not so for the dying. I'm sure if I tried, I could drum up some other people who are terminal. I have an oncologist after all. But summoning the dead for a little wisdom and advice is impossible. Those who have gotten the whole business over and done with are nowhere to be found, and they don't like to reach out.

Understandably, Graham and our girls are all focusing on the living—on *my* living, not on my dying. I know it's the only thing they can do, but it makes me even lonelier that I'm facing one direction, and they are looking the opposite way. It's like all our backs are turned on each other, which sounds much harsher than it is, since in reality we're doing no such thing.

Everyone's doing the very best they can, but people see what they want to, and denial is always a handy option.

Graham's refrain *Joan, think positive!* has become such a ubiquitous annoyance I'm afraid he's going to come home one day with custom-made T-shirts for all of us bearing the message printed in bright, neon letters. And sometimes, though not often, I want to scream at him, *It's about medicine, darling, not attitude!* But I know he knows that already, and he doesn't need my criticism to make worse that which is almost as bad as it can get, but not quite.

When the time comes for us to call hospice—angels walking among us—those people will have to split their efforts between both camps. I imagine them wearing two interchangeable hats throughout the days. First, focusing on the death side of their jobs monitoring my transition, controlling my pain and anxiety and keeping me clean, then nimbly switching to the life side, giving my family what they need to keep on living—kind reminders to eat, sleep, accept help, take breaks, put one foot in front of the other, grieve.

There's no way to know how long it will be, but I can tell that things are getting worse. My thinking, my moods, the strange sensations inside my head: it's in the brain now. I didn't think twice about cutting off the breast, but I'm terrified about losing my mind.

I'm trying to distract myself by being grateful. Our Christmas was lovely. We had the annual open house—Graham and the girls insisted—and not a single invited guest missed it. Christmas dinner was one of the best we've ever had—everyone said so—and if the gifts were a little more extravagant and if there were more of them than usual, it was for good reason.

I do wish Carolyn hadn't left college in the middle of her freshman year at Amherst to help. Graham and I can handle this. He and I can handle anything together. That's the only thing I would change if I could—well, one of them—her taking off all these past few months from school. But it's like I'm arguing with myself. Carolyn never fights back, but nor will she change her mind and allow my rants to persuade her that she doesn't need to be here, and that her being here won't influence the outcome.

I'm right about everything—both of us know it—but it hasn't impacted her decision or diminished her resolve to stay. And even though Anne has taken a leave from her job in Italy to be here too, I feel like I can lecture her even less than I can her younger sister. While I am glad to have my girls back home, I wish it wasn't at the expense of what's important in their lives. Of the three of them, Ceci is the most settled, and with a new baby, she's making her own family a priority instead of dropping everything in Boston to flock to my side, and I'm glad for that. She comes down when she can, and it's not time yet for her to come for the last time and stay till the end.

One thing I'm especially grateful for, because I wasn't sure he would visit when I invited him, was that Peter Herring, Anne's college boyfriend, came to see me right before Christmas. They've been split almost as long as they've been out of school—September will be two years—and he's with a lovely new young woman now who came with him.

If it had to be over with my daughter, I'm glad he's with someone I like. Who Peter loves has nothing to do with me, but we were such good friends when he and Anne were together. He already felt like family back then and I truly thought they would get married someday. They had plenty of time. He didn't have to, but my God, he shaved his head when I lost my hair—what twenty-one-year-old man does that?

And I always marveled that there was another man named Peter who loved a Cavanaugh woman.

I hadn't planned to share any of it with Peter, not even a little; it just happened the way it did. That December afternoon when we sat down to play chess like we always used to when he and Anne were together, I tried to feel out how he was about their split. It was the first time I'd seen him since it happened, and even though this was none of my business either, I felt like I should make amends on behalf of my daughter if I could, both for the break-up and for her terminating the pregnancy.

One thing about dying is you can get away with a lot more. Maybe not a felony, but you're liberated from certain etiquettes like beating around the bush. So once Peter and I started talking, I suggested he muster some forgiveness toward Anne. I thought it made some sense coming from me, since neither of us had known about her pregnancy before she ended it. Months after the fact, she revealed that decision to him, wielding it to make her break up with Peter cruelly absolute. And, when we went to her annual exam last year when she was home visiting from Italy, without intending to, I saw the number "one" that Anne had written on the line before the word abortion on the history form the receptionist asked her to update. That's how Peter and I each found out.

I realized too late that I should have stepped far more lightly. I could see on Peter's face that bringing up something so personal and painful had shamed him. I felt terrible. So to level the playing field, to try and repair having come on too strong, without a second thought I told him I'd been unfaithful when Graham and I were still newly married, and Ceci was a baby. When I had no idea what I was doing, walking around in the skin of my husband's wife and my child's mother.

It did the trick, I could tell. After I shifted my focus to my own shortcomings, Peter's relief was obvious. I didn't burden Peter with more details about the man than he needed to know. When he asked his name I told him, Hutch, short for his last name, Hutchinson, and the nickname he went by with everyone, and I said that as strange as it sounded, the dalliance had saved my marriage and helped me stay in a role that I'd been afraid I was going to fail at. That was the extent of what I said, and I thought that would be the end of it, but then Peter asked if I'd thought about finding Hutch to tell him I was sick. I told him I didn't want to talk about it anymore. He didn't push me, and we focused on the pieces on the board in front of us.

I wish I'd never found out, but I already knew where Hutch worked. The names of his wife and children. That he lived in New Canaan.

Almost four years ago, in 1985, his son Mark died in a car accident the night of his high school graduation, but when I first read the obituary, I didn't know if it was Hutch's son, or the boy of a stranger with the same name. Mark was seventeen, older than Carolyn and younger than Anne, and his younger sister Julia was a high school sophomore, the same as Carolyn. The ages of his children didn't prove or disprove anything, but the picture of Mark in the paper eliminated all doubts. There was no mistaking the uneven smile and the dark eyes he inherited from his father. Features I knew far better than I should have.

I had a terrible time getting through that summer. I was bereft that Hutch had lost his only son and that his family couldn't even grieve in private. The accident was in the papers and on the news. I strived to mimic the heartbreak of my friends who were parents saddened by the loss in a family so much like all of ours, but nonetheless a family they didn't know. Ceci had graduated from Williams the previous month, and Anne was getting ready to leave for her junior year in Italy that fall, so although I had the very real joys of my family to bolster me, and I did everything I could to stay busy, I was preoccupied by Hutch's loss and Mark's death. Then before Halloween that same year I got the cancer diagnosis, which scared me back into paying attention to my own life.

But on the day of Mark's funeral, with my family scattered in their own directions of work, friends, and the leisure of summer, I took the train to New Canaan and a taxi to Saint Aloysius. There had to be more than five hundred people, some shocked into silence, others weeping openly, all filing into the church and out of the relentless sun whose radiance that day was especially hard on the eyes. More than half of them were teenagers.

I wish I could say Hutch looked the same as he had twenty years earlier, but he didn't. Although he had aged well, his face bore the agony of a father who has lost a child and I hated seeing the transformation. Alice, his wife, and his daughter Julia, were two bowed figures in black who clung to him on either side. I slipped out of the church after twenty minutes and came home. I didn't belong there. I had no right to be among all those broken, grieving people who loved Mark and his family.

Just as I buried that sadness four years ago, I did what I needed to in order to stop Peter's questions during our chess game and end the discussion. But ever since his visit, I haven't been able to stop thinking about his suggestion—letting Hutch know I'm sick—so last night I wrote Peter a letter. It was late and I was tired, but I wanted to write it before I convinced myself not to. I sealed it in an envelope with his name on it and tucked it into one of my jewelry boxes. I won't look at it again.

28 February 1989

Dear Peter, I think I'm getting funny. This seems silly but I've thought about our visit, so I found him. Hutch. He has an office in the Trade Center. The girls and Graham are going to be going through enough so there's nothing I can do. But if you could, would you? If not, then never mind it. I'm glad I told you and thank you for giving Anne the forgiving. He's at Morgan Stanley, Hutch is. If you do it, you ask for Peter Hutchinson. Much love—J

Who knows if it's a risky thing to do. There's no way to know when or if Graham and the girls will find the envelope and if they do, if they'll send it to Peter, and if they do, if he'll do what I asked. Maybe my family will open it and Peter will never get it, and then what? Part of me thinks it's unfair and selfish and indulgent, but when I told Peter, no, I hadn't thought about telling Hutch, Peter said, *I'd want to know.* So I'm acting on *his* advice. That's what I keep reminding myself. The irony.

And more important than all those ifs that may or may not happen after I'm gone, I worry about the biggest if of all, which I'll take to my grave. I thank God, as equally as I repent, that Anne never had a genetic anomaly or medical complication.

By the grace of God, most of her features favor mine. Her eyes, that deep, chocolate brown, they're the giveaway, but you'd have to know what to look for. (Ceci's are blue, and Carolyn's are hazel.) I always said Anne got her great-grandfather's eyes because their dark hue in the few black and white photographs of him is suggestive enough. My grandfather—my mother's father—died young, when I was still a baby, and since I have no idea what color the man's eyes really were, it's possible that inherited trait is legitimately from him and not proof of my indiscretion. And while it's not obvious year-round, as soon as Anne gets in the sun she tans practically before your eyes, which neither of her sisters does nearly as quickly.

What would it mean, I wonder, when I lie in bed staring at the ceiling at two o'clock in the morning because of the steroids, if Hutch knew he had another child?

There's no question that Graham is as much Anne's father as he is Ceci's and Carolyn's, but I wish I could know if there will ever come a time when Anne learns that she is Peter Hutchinson's daughter. If that happens, I'll have no control over the aftermath. I can only hope that if the truth ever comes out, my family's anger won't fester and take on a life of its own.

More than that, I pray that they never question how fiercely I loved my husband and our lives together and the family we created. I made a mistake, but just as I knew I would never leave Graham, I always knew I would keep the baby—my Anne—as well as keep the truth from my husband, who I never meant to hurt. But during that time with Hutch—when I loved both men—I had so desperately needed to be seen. I felt invisible behind the curtains of marriage and motherhood and Hutch had seen me the way no one else had then, not even Graham.

And I was terrified he would leave me, not for the infidelity, which I would have begged him to forgive me for, and I could have imagined he would over time, but for having another man's baby. Although our marriage wasn't perfect, it had endured, but I couldn't imagine it remaining intact through a transgression that ruinous. And I wouldn't have been able to bear subjecting my child to the rejection and resentment that surely Graham would have felt toward her, even if he denied it, or tried to convince me that he didn't feel such things, and to masquerade as someone who didn't.

I've been thinking about God a lot lately, as you might imagine. I'm not afraid to die, I'm just not ready to go and I won't be there to tell Anne about a secret she deserves to know or persuade Graham that I did the only thing that I was truly capable of, even if it hadn't been the right thing, or the honest thing to do. God has been so good to my family—we have always been rich beyond measure in luck and love—and I pray that if His grace and blessings keep shining on them after I'm gone, those gifts will be compensation for my inability to make amends.

Joan Katherine Hamilton Cavanaugh
Beloved Wife and Mother
June 24, 1940-March 23, 1989

NEW YORK

1964

2

The first time Hutch saw Joan was on a frigid, icy, unforgiving Wednesday in February at the D'Agostino's around the corner from his grandmother's apartment. They were both twenty-three.

It's no defense of any kind, he knew then, and he knew later, but she didn't seem married. Hutch had graduated from Syracuse the previous spring and checking for a ring wasn't a skill he had thought to develop. There wasn't a need. Even though he had nothing at stake—not at the beginning—if he had the chance to do it all over again, he would have done things differently. This is a thought he's had for decades, like an affliction that can never be completely cured. Mostly, but not entirely.

Hutch and his grandmother, Margot, were very good friends. As the baby of the family, he remained her most devoted grandchild. All his siblings were married, and his brother and one sister had kids already, and his other sister was pregnant. Although his father had grown up in the apartment Margot still lived in, he and Hutch's mother both were much more comfortable in Rye. They never said it out loud, but Hutch sensed he and his grandmother both thought his parents were provincial. They simply weren't built for it, his mother never hesitated to explain in her recurring refrain: *We love going into the city, but your father and I just aren't built to live there.* But Margot was—she and his grandfather had raised Hutch's father and uncle there and had run their own business for forty years, a haberdashery that weathered the Depression because of the steadfastly loyal customers his grandparents cultivated. There was no home for Margot but the city.

Hutch benefitted from his siblings breaking in his parents and learned from them what pitfalls to avoid and what he could reasonably expect them to approve of, so after he graduated from college Hutch asked his father to give him a job while he decided what he wanted to do with an economics degree. In the same conversation, he offered to pay rent to sleep in his childhood bedroom. They agreed he'd work four days a week at his father's law office in White Plains. Hutch negotiated Wednesdays off to take a morning drawing class through the continuing education program at NYU. Hutch had minored in studio art because of the release valve the creativity provided, and how that offset the courses that required his mental immersion into the world of numbers and formulas. After graduation it remained a pursuit he wanted to return to. Those were the days Hutch visited Margot on the Upper East Side before taking the train home. He always called her after class let out to find out what the plan was. Some days they went out to lunch and on others they ate in her apartment.

No matter what they decided, Hutch always stopped at D'Agostino's beforehand to pick up flowers or dessert. Because of the terrible weather that afternoon, his grandmother told Hutch she would have lunch waiting on the table if he was sure he still wanted to join her, and to please be careful out in the snow and ice.

This is what Hutch remembered. Walking toward the bakery, he turned the corner at the end of an aisle and almost collided with a woman looking down at her shopping list.

"Sorry," Hutch said. "I beg your pardon."

"No, pardon me," the woman said. "Clearly I have to be as careful indoors as I do out in that mess."

She walked past him, and Hutch continued to the bakery and asked for a box of lady fingers.

When Hutch got to the register, the same woman was ahead of him in line, and he was able to get a better look at her. From what he could see she seemed very pretty but was wearing an unexpected bulky men's field coat, drab green, appropriate for the day but seemed like something she had borrowed from a stranger. While they waited, she twirled the ends of her dark blond hair that peeked out from a maroon knit cap. Their cashier was having trouble with the customer in front of the woman, a man who disagreed about what he was being charged for the roast he was buying, compared to what he said was advertised in the meat department. As a result, the cashier called for a manager to help handle the problem. The cashier was a meek woman, young, with hunched shoulders, who looked afraid to say anything to anyone. And the irate customer was a self-possessed older man in a suit and well-made overcoat who was having no trouble putting her in her place, only to find out that she hadn't made a mistake, but the advertised price of the meat was in error.

It was an uncomfortable exchange to witness: the sheepish cashier, the belligerent customer, the mediating manager. A long line had formed behind Hutch and the lines at all the registers were just as long with everyone in the neighborhood stocking up for the days of paralyzing, bad weather ahead. There was nothing to do but stand and wait until some resolution was reached and the man was on his way.

The woman turned around and took a step closer toward Hutch. One of her eyes was blue, the other, green. "You would think he could wait and have a fit on a day when there isn't a blizzard and there aren't so many of us in a hurry to get home." She didn't quite whisper it, like she wanted the man ahead of her to hear, and she didn't seem to recognize Hutch from their awkward exchange a few minutes earlier. "What a jerk." She smiled at Hutch like they were in on a dare together.

He was caught off guard and didn't know how to respond. He thought of kidding her about watching where she was going, almost running into people the way she did, but couldn't manage quickly enough on his feet. "Maybe he had a bad experience grocery shopping that he's never gotten over." He had spoken more quietly than she had and as soon as the words were out of his mouth, he wished he could take them back, but she laughed.

"Maybe he's a lonely man and this is the only chance he has to talk to people," she said.

"And this is how he always talks to people, which is why he's alone," Hutch said.

"Exactly!" She nodded and laughed. "That would explain a lot."

"Next please, miss, you're next!" The cashier called as Hutch watched the man walk toward the door of the store. The cashier waved the woman in front of him to unload her groceries.

"Oh, gosh, sorry," the woman said. Flustered, she stepped forward and emptied her basket on the conveyor belt and their line of shoppers advanced. "I'm sorry you had to deal with that clod. I was ready to say something to him then you called your manager. You shouldn't have to deal with that."

Whether she was shaken by the man or moved by the kindness of this woman, the cashier's eyes started to well up as she rang up the items and strived for composure. "Thank you for saying so," she said. "I apologize for the inconvenience of having to wait."

The woman spoke to the cashier, but she turned and smiled at Hutch. "It was no problem. We had some fun at his expense, right?" She paid and picked up her bag. "Thank you. You have to feel sorry for someone like that. Someone so angry," she said to the cashier. Then she looked at Hutch again. "Take care," she said, and she walked away.

It was only a few insignificant minutes of banter, but he was disappointed that it was over and that they couldn't go on talking and standing in line longer. She was funny and pretty and somehow in that short time, over something as irrelevant as a boorish customer, it felt like they had connected. After the cashier rang up Hutch's box of lady fingers, he left the store, and clutching the bag against his body, walked with his head bent against the snow and wind.

Margot's building was three long blocks from the market and when he got to the first curb and looked up, waiting for the light to change, he saw the woman—he saw her maroon hat—a block ahead of him. He crossed the street before the light changed and lengthened his stride as much as he could to close the lead she had on him, which was difficult on the slick sidewalk. He was getting closer, but before he could catch her, she turned and walked into his grandmother's building—the very one where Hutch was headed—but by the time he walked into the lobby, it was empty.

There was nothing for it. He could have asked his grandmother about the woman, but he didn't want to regret initiating a subject she might then bring up every week. *Did you find out who she was?* She might ask, *Your mystery lady?* The question had the potential to be an unpleasant reminder that he'd lost the woman before he'd even had her. *No, Gran,* Hutch would have to say, *The trail's still cold.* The futility of the imagined conversation sounded so clear, even in his head, there was no question that he was going to keep his mouth shut. While Hutch waited for the elevator, he examined the names on the mailboxes in the lobby wondering which one belonged to her. That afternoon when his grandmother asked him what was new, he only told her about what they were working on in class and gave the same report about his father's office that he did every time she asked.

Every Wednesday for the next two months he shopped at D'Ag's, both before and after he visited Margot. If the woman lived in the same building, he was confident she had to return to her neighborhood grocery store to shop again, and soon. Unless she was a visitor, like Hutch was, and so would be there less frequently, if at all, and possibly never.

He didn't see her again until an afternoon in early April, when he was waiting for the elevator in his grandmother's lobby. When it arrived and the doors opened, the woman walked out pushing a baby in a stroller. She smiled at him as she passed Hutch, but she didn't say anything. He wondered, *Why was she with a baby? Was the baby hers? Was she a nanny or babysitter?* It threw him off; if she'd been alone, he would have tried to pick up where they'd left off months earlier, *Hello again! From the line at D'Ags during that storm? You almost ran into me, remember?* Instead, he was left with the same two options to answer these new questions: asking his grandmother or lurking in the market, hoping their paths would cross again. And for what? Another five minutes of clever chatter? She was just a girl and there were girls everywhere. He was delusional to think they needed to finish something that had been so superficial.

It wasn't until a month later, the first week in May, that he saw her again. Hutch and Margot had taken a walk in Central Park and were going back to her apartment; the woman was walking toward them, pushing the baby in the stroller again. The baby wore a yellow sunhat.

"Hello, Margot," she said to his grandmother, and then she smiled at Hutch. "We meet again."

This, he hadn't expected.

"How are you, Joan? This is my grandson, Peter," his grandmother said.

He extended his hand, and he and Joan shook. "It's a pleasure to meet you," he said. "Hutch. Everyone calls me Hutch. She's the only one who calls me Peter, really." He angled his head toward his grandmother.

"Okay, Hutch. Likewise. It's nice to put a name with the face." Joan said to Margot, "We've seen each other in the neighborhood a few times."

That was the beginning of the beginning, while Hutch's grandmother leaned over the stroller and cooed at the baby. "Hello, Ceci you sweet, sweet girl." She reached down and squeezed the baby's left foot. Ceci smiled. "Such a darling." She stood up and touched Joan's elbow. "And how are you doing?"

"We're having a good day so far," Joan said. "Although most days I'm not really sure what I'm doing. It's very often touch-and-go." Her words contradicted her chirpy tone. She could have been reciting a nursery rhyme whose uplifting words had been replaced with desperate ones.

"Oh, sweetheart, none of us did," his grandmother said. "You figure it out, by the hour sometimes. She's so happy, that's how you can tell. That's how you know you're doing a good job. If you have a happy baby you're doing things right."

So her name was Joan, and Ceci, the baby, was her baby.

This conversation with his grandmother about motherhood was common ground for them, and a topic to which Hutch had nothing to contribute. Their commiserating made him invisible. After a few minutes, Hutch and Margot continued on their way back to her apartment while Joan pushed the stroller in the opposite direction, deeper into the park.

"They're such a nice couple." His grandmother looked at him then, as if she'd made a discovery. "They're about your age, I think. Her husband, Graham, he's in law school. I should have you all over for lunch or something," she said. "Help you make some friends in the city. They just live one floor up, on nine. Yes, I think you'd really hit it off with them."

So there it all was: everything he'd wanted to know, plus an opportunity, a way into these strangers' lives—except now there wasn't just Joan, the woman (and mother) whose identity he'd longed to discover, but also her baby, Ceci, and her husband, Graham, too. It wasn't what Hutch had hoped for. He was relieved he'd never said anything to his grandmother.

In that moment, like a reflex, he took his frustration out on his grandmother, who was blameless and kind. "Don't go wasting your time on my social life Gran," Hutch said, too sharply. "People don't connect simply because they're the same age. If you want us all over, I'll come, of course, but please don't work too hard. I have enough friends."

He wasn't surprised she was quietly defensive. "I take care of my family, Peter. That's not wasting my time. I have nice neighbors and I have a nice grandson who might benefit from a friendship with my nice neighbors. Suit yourself. Now you know where to find them."

Ultimately his grandmother dropped it, and chastened, Hutch didn't say anything more either.

That seemed to be the end of it until a week later, when Hutch was leaving Margot's apartment. The elevator door opened, and Joan and Ceci were already inside.

"Hello, Hutch," Joan said. "How are you? I was thinking of asking your grandmother about you. Are you doing anything right now? Would you like to walk with us?"

And that was the real beginning.

If Hutch was looking for a friend, a young, married woman with a baby was hardly the best choice, but it always felt like Joan had pursued him instead of the other way around. And certainly it had to be that way, didn't it? She was the married one, she had more to risk, to lose. And although Hutch should have had far better judgment, and much more restraint, he was no agent of morality. If she was unhappy in her marriage, that unhappiness preceded Hutch—that's what he told himself. A happy marriage can't be intruded on by a third party.

And if he was being honest, that she might find him worthy of being unfaithful with transformed his sense of self-importance. His self-esteem, his whole regard for who he thought he was before, changed because of her. Maybe, because of Hutch, Joan saw her marriage as a mistake she could extract herself from. He wasn't proud of what happened, but he never took it lightly.

It didn't happen according to his grandmother's plan, but Hutch did become friends with her neighbor. Starting that first afternoon, they walked every Wednesday after he'd visited Margot, and except for Ceci, they may as well have been two single people alone together. Yet, when other people passed them, smiled and said hello, Hutch didn't mind if they thought the three of them were a family.

They each talked about their friends, then Joan's four sisters, and Hutch's brother and sisters, and their parents and college and the city and his drawing class at NYU. They didn't talk about Graham or her marriage. Joan was a great reader and when she told him about *The Group*, a *New York*

Times bestseller she was reading and loved and couldn't put down, he said he'd get a copy so they could discuss it, and Joan laughed. After he'd bought the book and started reading it, he understood why she had laughed, but he was intrigued by the characters and the world they occupied. The people, the women in particular, Hutch realized, he knew nothing about. It was an eye-opener.

At first, they arranged to meet at a specific bench in the park at three o'clock after Hutch's visit with Margot, and walk from there. Hutch suggested it and Joan agreed. He needed the concrete break between the time he spent with Margot and the time he spent with Joan—they were such disparate visits that going from one to the other was disorienting and he needed a chance between them to switch roles. In the one he was a child, an adult child certainly, but still the child of his grandmother's own child, and in the other he was a man who had befriended a married woman, but not her husband. He needed time between the two people, both of whom he was, and both of which were true, to metamorphose between them. To shift from Hutch the grandson, the boy, to Hutch, the suitor? The complication? He wasn't sure what he was to Joan, but he was certainly a different version of himself when he was with her than when he was with his grandmother.

Hutch hated when people were late. It had been instilled early in him by his father, a man who was intolerant of anyone's tardiness, but most especially his children's. It may have been a gamble after their first walk to expect Joan to meet him at exactly the time they'd agreed on. She had a child after all, whose sleeping and eating and changing schedule Joan herself was at the mercy of, and by extension—as he waited for the two of them—Hutch was, too. So he gave her a lot of latitude, and for that first month she had never been more than fifteen minutes late. It gave Hutch more time to shift from one mode of himself to another and it wasn't a problem.

But in early June, the fifth time they were supposed to meet, fifteen minutes went by, then twenty and twenty-five until after forty-five minutes Hutch wasn't sure whether to go and check on her or just get on the train and go home. While he was still deciding, he heard a woman's voice.

"Peter Hutchinson, what in the world?"

When he looked up, he recognized a woman he'd gone to high school with, Madeleine Martin, walking toward him. He couldn't remember when or where exactly he'd seen her since graduation. Someone's Christmas party? A bonfire on the beach last summer? She wasn't someone he had been interested in; she wasn't smart or clever or funny enough, but he remembered that she had liked him, and he'd felt guilty that he hadn't just put his criticisms aside and gone out with her to find out that maybe he was mistaken. She was very pretty, with a dimple that appeared both when she smiled and spoke, and it might have been easy to give in and simply be adored by someone even if he didn't feel the same way, at least not at first.

Madeleine looked at him as if she'd made a fabulous discovery. She pressed her palms together and looked right and left and over both shoulders as if she expected someone else to appear out of thin air and beat her to what she'd found: Hutch sitting alone on a bench.

He stood up, looking in the direction he expected to see Joan, who still was not showing.

"Hello, Madeleine," he said. He bent at the waist in a small, satirical bow. "Stating the obvious, 'fancy meeting you here.' It's sure been a while, huh? What brings you to my bench this afternoon?"

Madeleine looked at him, genuinely confused. "Sorry, what do you mean 'your bench'? I'm going to get coffee for my boss."

He was instantly reminded why they wouldn't have lasted more than a week—and that was being generous. "Never mind, I'm just kidding. That was dumb." Hutch shook his head and waved his hand. "I'm waiting for a friend who is very late, and I was trying to figure out what to do. I didn't expect to run into anyone I know. You caught me off guard."

Madeleine smiled, seeming to appreciate the explanation for his failed humor. "Well, then how about coming to get a cup of coffee with me if your friend is a no-show? We could catch up a little." Her delight made him uncomfortable.

Hutch cocked his head to consider Madeleine's offer and his options for refusing when he heard his name and looked and saw Joan and Ceci coming toward them. Joan was jogging, pushing the stroller in front of her, and Ceci, red-faced and buckled in, fists balled, was screaming, arching her back and kicking her feet.

"Hutch! Hutch!" Joan waved. "I'm so sorry!"

As she got closer and slowed down and then stopped in front of them, Hutch could see that Joan had also been crying. She sat down on the bench, next to the stroller, breathing heavily.

He turned to Madeleine and shrugged. "Thank you anyway, Madeleine, but here's my friend after all."

Madeleine's expression shifted. She was no longer smiling, and her dimple disappeared. She cupped her chin in her left hand, and her fingers covered her mouth.

"I am so sorry, Hutch," Joan said quietly, looking at the ground, catching her breath. "Really, I didn't expect you to still be here."

"Well, then." Madeleine repeated the same first two words she'd just uttered, but this time far more loudly to compete with Ceci's crying, and also with a cold, hard edge that Hutch interpreted as judgment, or at the very least, disapproval. She slid her fingers away from her mouth, but kept her chin in her hand, seeming to ponder the situation. After a long look—too long Hutch thought—at him and Joan and Ceci wailing in the stroller, she said, "It was nice running into you anyway, Hutch. Take care."

"Yeah, you, too," said Hutch. And then, for lack of a better, obvious option to end their exchange and send her on her way, added, "Good luck, Madeleine."

Madeleine walked away and Hutch sat down next to Joan, who was wiping her eyes with a tissue. "She wouldn't go down for a nap and then she wouldn't stop crying because she was overtired, and I didn't know if I should stay and keep trying or just forget the whole thing and come see you anyway. I was certain you'd be gone," Joan said. "God, what an awful fucking mess I am."

"Come on," said Hutch. "No you're not. That's a lot. You're okay. Let's walk. I'll push her and you can tell me more about it, if you want. You saved me from an extraordinary waste of time, by the way. I'm really glad you came. I was worried you wouldn't."

After that day they abandoned the park plan and developed a new system, which Joan devised. Hutch was happy to give up his solitary transition time to make things easier for her. On Wednesdays, Joan's signal for him to come pick her and Ceci up for a walk was a piece of string she tied around the knob of her front door. Only twice during their time together there was no string. The first time, after Hutch got off the elevator and rounded the corner and saw the doorknob—no string—he pivoted and started back for the elevator.

Behind him, he heard a door open, and a man's voice call out, "Be back in a flash, darling." And Graham left their apartment and joined Hutch and they both waited for the elevator.

Maybe Graham was surprised to see a stranger waiting for the elevator on his floor when he got there, maybe not. Hutch and Graham nodded to each other, and in his panic Hutch feigned an attitude of being as entitled to be there as Graham was. When the elevator arrived, Graham gestured for Hutch to enter first and after they rode down to the lobby in silence, Hutch offered Graham the chance to exit before him. After Graham left the building, Hutch walked around the corner in the opposite direction, stopped and squatted with his back resting against the concrete wall until his heart stopped racing.

The second time, as soon as Hutch saw there was no string, he sprinted to the stairwell, took the steps down two at a time, raced out of the building, and for the next three blocks, ran like a man being chased.

On a hot July 1st, he knocked on her door like he had for the past few weeks, but when Joan opened it, she put her finger to her lips and whispered, *She's sleeping,* and Hutch whispered back, *Sorry I'll go,* and Joan had said, *No, don't. Please stay,* and for the first time, took his hand in hers and led him into the apartment, and into her bedroom, and closed the door behind her.

Although Hutch wasn't inexperienced, the longest he had been with the same woman was for two months his junior year in college. Her name was Helen, and while Hutch had been crazy about her because she was beautiful and funny and smart and a good athlete who played on Syracuse's women's varsity tennis team—he played on the men's—she didn't enjoy their sex as much as Hutch did, so he was conflicted and confused about how, if at all, to improve that part of their relationship. She liked him and was affectionate and was a fabulous date at parties, but bashful and modest, albeit accommodating, when it came to sex.

Hutch finally grew so uncomfortable about their dynamic in the bedroom (he and his roommate negotiated their private uses of their room on a schedule around both their girlfriends) that he couldn't keep up the belief that anything was going to improve, and that with time Helen would become enthusiastic. After he ended the relationship, gently, Helen didn't seem remotely hurt, or to even mind, and in fact, Hutch thought she appeared relieved. She was as friendly to him as she'd always been, the way she'd been before they started dating, and Hutch almost felt like their intimate connection had never happened.

When it came to sex, Joan was the opposite of Helen.

That summer day, Joan walked him over to the bed, pressed her hand against the back of his neck, pulled him toward her and kissed him. Her other hand grazed the front of his pants.

Finally, Hutch said, "Joan, look what you're doing to me. Are you sure?"

Joan stepped away from him and started to undress. "Yes, Hutch," she said. "Shh." After she was naked, she undressed him.

He realized he hadn't known what to expect, and once she was standing in front of him naked, he was in awe at what a marvel she was. He had never seen this intimately, let alone slept with, a woman who had given birth. He had heard his sisters lament about baby weight and lost waistlines after their children were born, but that was a different thing entirely and not one he paid close attention to, nor wished to. Joan had a small waist with a little paunch below it, which he interpreted as both proof of the child she'd had as well as her body's determined return to the one it had been before it had housed a growing baby.

She shyly pushed him down on the bed and eased herself on top of him. "I think about you every day," she whispered. "I have been wanting this for a long time."

Afterward, Hutch lay on top of her, propped on his elbows. They gazed at each other in silence for several minutes until Hutch finally spoke.

"My God, you are so wonderful," he said.

They didn't always go to bed. There was one afternoon when Joan opened the door on the verge of tears, pale, with dark circles under her eyes.

"I was up with her all night," she said. "Can you watch her while I lie down for a few minutes please?"

After she handed Ceci to Hutch, Joan got into bed and burrowed under the covers. He didn't know anything about babies—the only babies he'd held, and briefly, were his brother's and sister's kids—but she seemed so desperate that, in lieu of being an expert, Hutch only had to be competent. Joan's daughter was the first baby he was independently left in charge of. Ceci seemed curious about him, but not alarmed, and they walked around the apartment while he pointed at things quietly saying their names, asking her questions she couldn't answer, standing in front of the windows and talking about the city, the buildings, the cars on the street and the tiny people walking. She didn't cry and she didn't laugh, but she seemed content.

After forty-five minutes she put her head on Hutch's shoulder, which made him afraid to move at all, but after she kept it there for more than ten minutes, he went into her room and managed to sit in the rocker until even he recognized the unmistakable breathing of a sleeping baby. He put Ceci in her crib and tiptoed into Joan's bedroom. She was sleeping as deeply as her daughter, and Hutch let himself out of the apartment, locking the door behind him.

On a handful of afternoons, he sketched her. The first one he did at school, from memory, and Joan was embarrassed when he showed it to her, saying there was no way she really looked like that, so he asked her to pose for him so he could get her right—those were the words he used—and she did. The one time he drew her naked, that was her idea.

Hutch never viewed Graham as an adversary or rival. There was nothing to be gained from it. Graham was a factor over which he had no control but who prevented certain outcomes, the way a thunderstorm disrupts plans for a picnic. Hutch was at the mercy of the weather in Joan's marriage and there was nothing to be done but adapt. He was determined to be grateful for the happiness he'd been afforded and not be greedy for more. When holidays and summer plans interrupted their schedule, they didn't discuss anything beyond agreeing on the date of their next visit.

On the train home, when, toward the end, Hutch's frustration began to encroach on his happiness, he found hollow comfort in a certain self-criticism: *Would you rather not know her at all? What if there were no Joan?* As tenuous as those afternoons were, they were, he knew, far better than anything else he'd ever had with a woman.

Although they never talked about Graham, there was no forgetting, every time Hutch undressed Joan and kissed her neck and let her press him against her kitchen counter, that it was all happening in the man's own home. In the beginning he was prepared for Joan to bring him up, but after enough time had passed and she never did, Hutch understood that Graham was a topic that was off-limits.

There was only one time they came close to talking about him. It had been a little over a year since he had seen her for the first time in D'Agostino's. Joan had made him a drink, which she handed to Hutch as soon as he was inside the apartment.

"Sit," she said. She laid her hand against his shoulder, guiding him into the living room where she already had her own drink on a coaster on the table in front of the couch. When she sat down, she tucked one leg under her, picked up her drink, took a sip and said, "Darling, how was your day at the office?" The way she said it sounded like a joke was coming, one that Hutch wasn't in on. She smiled, playful, waiting.

He took a sip of his drink and ran his other hand over his mouth and chin. He didn't know where this was going and didn't like that he didn't know. "What are you talking about?" Hutch said.

"I know. I'm ridiculous, aren't I?" She laughed but looked embarrassed. "I was just trying to be playful and fun. I'm sorry."

What had that been for her? A test? A way to feel out how he'd answer such a contrived question? He had no idea, but that afternoon Hutch knew that he had to end it. That cold, hard fact struck him because the truth was, he had imagined his life with her and *their* baby in *their* apartment but in his gut he knew it was never going to happen. As deep as Hutch was in, getting in any deeper would have only made things worse.

For the next week, he tried to figure out how to do it. He couldn't send a letter. He could risk calling during their regular Wednesday time hoping she would answer, but that was a coward's solution. Hutch simply wanted to avoid seeing her face when he told her. He didn't know what he was more afraid of: anger or sorrow or relief, but there wasn't a good choice among them, and it was selfish that he didn't want to witness a single one.

So on that last Wednesday, when he got to her apartment, the string was there. This time after she opened the door Hutch was the one who put his hand against the small of her back and guided her to her couch and said, "Joanie, let's sit."

She did and the way her shoulders drooped, and her face fell, Hutch could tell that she knew what was coming even before he said the words.

"I'm in love with you, and I've got nowhere to go with that," he said. "*We* can't go anywhere from here. Just this, there's only this, and I can't anymore. Having only this much of you—" he held up a tiny space between his right index finger and thumb—"is not enough."

Joan sat on the couch with her head in her hands. Her body shook while she cried. "You're right. I'm sorry, I'm sorry. I'm just so sorry, Hutch."

He kissed her forehead and smelled her hair and left her sitting on her couch with her hands covering her face, sobbing. He called his grandmother and begged off for the next month. His class had ended, he told her, which was true, and he had started working on Wednesdays at his father's office, which wasn't yet true but would be. After a month, he switched his visits to Saturday mornings and wore a hat and sunglasses which he didn't wear as a disguise so much as a barrier.

The one time Hutch needed the hat and sunglasses, though, he wasn't wearing them. The elevator opened on his grandmother's floor and the three of them were on it. Joan behind Ceci in the stroller, Graham next to Joan with his hand against the small of her back. Hutch had no choice but to join them. They all said hello like friendly strangers, Graham's voice louder and cheerier than Joan's and Hutch's, and they rode to the lobby in a silence that felt like a mockery and Hutch realized it was the second time he and Graham had taken that ride together.

Although Joan never saw Hutch again, as far as he knew, he spent the next month spying on the building for a glimpse of her, alone or not, it didn't matter. He'd come full circle, behaving like he'd gone back in time. He had to abandon the affair, but he wasn't prepared to never see her again. During those weeks, he only saw her twice: once, alone, pushing Ceci in the stroller, and once walking with another woman, a friend maybe, or one of her sisters. He'd imagined the comfort seeing her would give him, but it delivered the opposite: proof of what he was missing, what he never should have had, and the taunt that he'd never find the same thing with another woman who didn't already belong to someone else.

The saner part of him knew he had to interrupt the cycle of desperation and his staying in New York made that unlikely. Hutch told his parents he was ready for a change and asked his father to call in a favor from a lawyer friend in Philadelphia who gave him a job and he moved. A client who was a banker liked his work, and before the end of the year he was working at Boenning & Scattergood.

Eighteen months later Margot had a stroke, which no one had seen coming because of her seemingly good health, and which she didn't survive. Besides losing his grandmother—his dear friend—Margot's death also represented the irrefutable finality of the end of his time with Joan.

Hutch had ended it on Joan's couch in her living room, and he had left New York and taken control of his life and started with a blank slate in another city. He hadn't looked back. But subconsciously he'd allowed that, as long as his grandmother and Joan lived in the same building, there remained the faint and unrealistic chance, a possibility.

With Margot's death, Hutch's hopes, flimsy as they were, died too.

3

There was a period of time early in their marriage, when Ceci was a little over a year old, when Joan wasn't herself. She seemed like she was somewhere else much of the time. Graham couldn't put his finger on it, and he didn't bother to figure out why. It's not something he's proud of.

Then, sometime within that year, the distance she'd forged between them—that unnamed and gradual divide—disappeared and she was back to being the woman she'd always been. His love. His life. His home. His wife.

They had gotten married so young, two weeks after they graduated from St. Lawrence, where they'd been serious since junior year (he was on the varsity ice hockey team and Joan was a Larriette; she was as strong a skater as Graham was) and then Joan was pregnant right away. After four years in that isolated and insulated environment, being thrust into their lives in the city was an adjustment for them both. There was a trust, left by Graham's grandfather—for the only child of his only child—designated for the sole purpose of purchasing his first home. That summer they bought their apartment on the Upper East Side. Their first and only home.

They had met in 1961 in the bar of the Holiday Inn where the hockey team and Larriettes were staying after the Saints had defeated Cornell 7-0 at an away game at Lynah Rink in Ithaca. Graham's buddy, Richie Broadbelt, the team's goalie, liked Joan, and had devised a plan for him and Graham to join Joan and another Larriette, Judy Roberts, at the table where they were sitting.

"Maybe Judy's not what you're looking for," Richie had said. "But can you just talk to her tonight while I try and make some progress with Joan? I'll make it up to you."

The team had trounced the Big Red and the atmosphere in the bar was victorious and loud and smoky. Graham had nothing to lose and nothing at stake and said, "Sure, Rich, why not?"

They approached the table where the girls were sitting and Richie said, "Good evening, ladies, may we join and celebrate with you? We sure clobbered them, didn't we?"

Both of them laughed and Richie sat down next to Joan, and Graham sat across from him next to Judy.

Joan pointed at Graham. "You're in my sociology class. With Dr. Auster. You doodle too much."

Judy giggled and covered her mouth and both Richie and Graham looked at each other not quite sure what to say. Richie shrugged, seeming to realize before Graham did, this early defeat, and that tonight he wasn't going to be the one who had a chance with Joan.

"Yeah, I'm in Auster's class," Graham said. "I didn't know you were, too."

Joan tilted her head with authority. "I get there early and sit a few rows behind you. You usually come in late, and you always sit in the same row. When *I'm* bored, I watch you doodle."

"You watch me doodle when you're bored?" Graham laughed. "How am I supposed to respond to that? Maybe I'll have to start sitting behind you."

"Come on. Don't do that," said Joan. She smiled at him. "You should be flattered. If they weren't any good, I wouldn't keep watching you. I especially like when you do Snoopy."

Richie spoke up. "Does anyone else want another drink? I'm getting one."

The three of them said yes and Richie left the table.

After he left, Joan looked at Judy, then at Graham. "Listen, I know he wants to ask me out and I'm just not interested," she said. "He's talked to me before at practices, but I've just been delaying the inevitable since he hasn't directly asked me out. I don't know what he thought bringing you over would do." She pointed at Graham again. "I'm glad you guys won tonight but your being his wingman or whatever doesn't change anything. In the meantime, let's be kind."

Graham didn't know how to answer, and there wasn't time to respond before Richie was back with all their drinks, so Graham walked back to the bar and asked the bartender if he had a deck of cards, and he did.

"Crazy," the bartender said, "No one has ever asked me for cards before. I just have them to play solitaire when it's slow."

So the four of them played hearts and drank until it was late and time to go back to their rooms. And when they left the bar, after all those hours had passed, Joan and Graham walked together, and Richie walked with Judy.

Graham said good night to Joan in the hallway outside her room at one o'clock in the morning. "I had such a wonderful time with you tonight," he said. "I'd like to call you when we get back to school." It felt underhanded not to square things with Richie first.

"You do that," said Joan. She rested her hand against his chest, leaned forward and kissed him. "And I think you probably know what I'm going to say."

At their wedding, Richie had given a toast and said, "To the lovely and bewitching Joan, and my dear old pal and teammate Graham. My wedding gift was introducing the two of you the night you met, officially anyway, junior year the night we beat Cornell. I'm glad it worked out for one of us, friend." He lifted his glass to the bride and groom, then pivoted to include rest of the reception. "To the Cavanaughs!"

After Graham started law school in September at Columbia, did his life revolve around classes and studying? As a reward and release for his hard work, did he drink too much on the weekends and at parties just like he had in college? Was he self-absorbed? Did he spend too little time with his pregnant wife, and later, his wife and baby? Did he drive her away from the center of their marriage rather than toward it? Graham knew the honest answers to all those questions he asked himself, but what he suspected and feared about Joan, he didn't want confirmed.

Given his preoccupation with succeeding in school, the hours he spent working and worrying about who was doing better than he was, it's a wonder he noticed the piece of string, tied in a bow around the doorknob of their front door, one afternoon during those months when Joan was distant and removed.

At the end of the day, Graham came home, dropped his books on the table in the kitchen and asked Joan to come back out to the foyer.

"Why is that string there?" he said. "Have you seen this? Where did this come from?" Joan watched while Graham pulled one end of the string to untie it then stared at it dangling between his thumb and index finger. She cocked her head and kept staring at his hand holding the string, but her expression was blank. She crossed her arms.

"I have no idea," she said finally. "What a strange thing." Then she turned her gaze away from Graham's hand and looked him in the eye. "You know what? I think it's those Wilson kids. You know the ones, Barbara's nephews who come visit?" Barbara lived on ten, the floor above them. "I've seen them more than once running around the building, riding the elevator for fun. One day they had string and scissors and were fooling around by people's doors."

"Did you say something to them?" Graham said.

"No," said Joan. "Ceci was overdue for her nap and she was screaming, and I wasn't really paying attention at the time. I had my hands full. I'm just remembering it now."

"What a strange thing to do," he said. "Really, what's the point? It's kind of stupid, isn't it? And I don't see string on anyone else's door."

Joan shrugged. "Who knows? They're odd kids. Always a little off, I thought," she said. "Maybe other people just pay more attention to their doorknobs and took their strings off before we ever even noticed ours."

Graham thought that had been the end of it, but a few days later, when he got home Joan met him at the door. She had started cooking, pots were already heating on the stove, but she needed butter, could he run out to D'Ag's and pick some up? She kissed him hello and walked with her arm in his to wait for the elevator. After she'd pushed the button she leaned her head against his shoulder.

"How was your day?" she said. "Do you have a lot of work tonight? Oh, will you look at that? I'll be darned."

She unlinked her arm from Graham's and walked down the hall to not one but two other apartments' doors—the Murrays' and the Coughlins'—and pointed at the knobs which both had pieces of string tied around them, both of which she took off. Barely noticeable Graham thought, practically impossible to see from where he stood in front of the elevator.

"They're up to it again," Joan said. "See? Just like ours." She seemed satisfied to have uncovered evidence that supported Barbara's visiting nephews' bad behavior. She shook her head and walked back to Graham, waving the strings like she was ringing a dinner bell.

"Thanks for getting the butter," she said. "See you in a minute."

She left him waiting in the hall and starting walking back to their apartment.

"Joan," Graham said, and she stopped and looked at him. "I don't know how in the world you saw those strings from here. I couldn't see them."

"I just did," she said. "So I don't know how in the world you *didn't* see them."

She went back to the apartment and Graham went to the store and bought the butter.

There were no more strings on anyone's doorknobs after that, but there were other oddities that Graham thought curious only after the fact.

There had been a man waiting for the elevator on their floor one afternoon, about Graham's age, someone he'd never seen before, and didn't see again until many months later when he, Joan and Ceci were headed out to breakfast one Saturday morning in April and the same man had gotten on when the elevator stopped on the eighth floor, one down from theirs. They'd all said hello, but afterward Joan was quiet, and Graham waited to see how and when her mood changed.

After they left the building, the man went in the opposite direction and the three of them walked down the sidewalk in silence: Joan pushing Ceci in the stroller, Graham beside Joan. For three blocks they walked like that—the restaurant was five blocks away—and it wasn't until they ran into Ken and Olivia—friends of friends they hadn't seen since a

Christmas party they all attended the previous December—that Joan snapped out of it.

When he looked back on that brief rocky time, Graham wondered if it had been depression that she'd had, postpartum, although people didn't talk about that in those days. Whatever had been going on for Joan during that period, if it was related to having a new baby, the same thing didn't happen again with the other two girls, and once she seemed past it, Graham was just relieved and grateful that it was over.

Then when she was pregnant with Anne, she didn't tell him right away, as soon as she was late, not like she did with Ceci.

"How late are you," he asked, expecting her to say what she had before: *Late enough, almost two weeks. And I can tell, Graham, I just know.*

But that wasn't what she said at the end of April when she finally told him.

"A little over ten weeks," Joan said.

She smiled at him, but Graham was hurt and confused. "What? You should have told me sooner," he said. "Why didn't you?"

"You know Bridget's neighbor, the one she plays tennis with? Christine?" she said. Bridget was one of Joan's four sisters.

"I don't know," Graham said. "Do I know a single goddamn thing about Bridget's neighbor?"

"Christine," Joan said the woman's name again. "I have mentioned her to you. Anyway, when I first thought I was late, Bridget told me Christine had miscarried for the second time in a year, and it scared me. I just worried about saying something too soon. I know it's superstitious, but we were so lucky with Ceci I thought maybe twice was pushing our luck. I didn't want to jinx anything. I'm sorry, Graham."

Her explanation didn't satisfy him or make him any less hurt. "I don't think telling your husband qualifies as saying something too soon or jinxing anything."

"I know," she said. "I am sorry. Aren't you happy now that you know? I hope you are. I am." She smiled again. "It's the very best news."

"Of course I'm happy," he said. "But Joan, surely if something had happened, if you had miscarried, wouldn't you have told me? Wouldn't I have found out then? That there was a pregnancy, but wasn't any more?"

"Yes, of course I would have told you," she said. "Let's stop talking about this sad, sad stuff, can we please? I really am sorry. We're so lucky and everything is fine. Don't worry, Graham. Everything is going to be okay."

As convincing as he knew Joan thought she was, Graham hadn't bought the story about the string on their doorknob for a minute. He hadn't bought it to the point where one Sunday afternoon after he'd seen Barbara's nephews in the lobby, he went to her apartment and knocked on the door with ten pieces of string he'd cut from the roll in their kitchen drawer, the lengths of which could easily be tied around as many doorknobs in the building.

"Hello Graham," Barbara said when she opened the door. "What can I do for you?"

"I'm actually here to see your nephews," he said. "I found something that I think belongs to them."

Neither Joan nor Graham knew Barbara well, only that she'd been married for a short time before she and her husband divorced. One of the results of her never remarrying or having children of her own seemed to be that she doted on her brother's two sons.

She invited him in and called the boys to the foyer. Contrary to what Joan said, Graham didn't think they were more odd or different than any other boys their ages, which were about ten and eight, he guessed. Barbara introduced the three of them. The older one was named Everett, the younger one was Michael.

"I don't want to get you two in any kind of trouble, but I did want to return something that I believe belongs to you," Graham said. He reached into his coat pocket and pulled out the pieces of string, which had since morphed from ten neat parallel lines on his kitchen counter into a tangled wad of no significance. Graham held out his right palm with the mess of string toward Michael, who was standing closer to him. Michael looked baffled and didn't extend his own hand to take what Graham offered. He continued to hold out his hand in the awkward space between them. Michael looked at his brother and then at Graham. Neither of them said anything.

"I know there are all kinds of ways to have fun in a boring apartment building when you have to come visit your aunt," Graham said. His displaced anger and frustration bled into his script designed to shame and intimidate the boys into admitting what Joan told him they had done. In his gut Graham suspected they had no idea what he was talking about, but he would have welcomed their confession with a relief he'd never known before.

Then he baited them with a lie of his own: "My cousin and I actually used to do the same thing in his building when I would visit him."

"I'm sorry, Mr. Cavanaugh," Everett said. Although he was farther from Graham than Michael was, being older he stepped in on behalf of them both seeming ready to clear their names and set the record straight. "I don't know why you think that string belongs to us."

Although the boys' confusion validated what he suspected—that Joan had made up the story to rationalize the string's appearance on their own doorknob—the fact that this exchange was proving his suspicion correct was accompanied by a sense of extreme discomfort. He hadn't expected the boys to agree to doing what Joan had claimed, but he had clung to the slim hope, the outside chance, that he was wrong, the very opposite of what he spent every day in law school trying to establish—how right he was. He'd never been a gambler and against his better judgment, panicked about his marriage, Graham placed a bad bet that day that they would sheepishly confirm the story Joan had told him.

"Tying pieces of string around doorknobs in the building?" Graham said. "You two haven't been doing that after you've run out of other games to play when you're stuck here?" He didn't want to solely indict Joan to these boys and Barbara, so he added another lie to the pile. "After I found string around my doorknob, I asked some other people in the building if they knew anything about it and several claimed they saw the two of you putting them on other doorknobs. On more than one floor."

Graham's anger at Joan was landing on these poor kids. Even when he thought he had come to the end of it, there was more.

The boys continued to look baffled, wearing the classic expressions of the wrongly accused. Graham dropped his extended arm and it hung dumbly next to his body, the string still wadded in his palm, growing damp.

Barbara tried to intervene. "Boys, what matters right now is that you're honest if what Mr. Cavanaugh says is true. You won't be punished for telling the truth. It's a harmless thing you did."

The boys' trembling lips gave away they were about to cry. It would have been obvious to anyone that their response was out of persecution or frustration or anger but not guilt. They hadn't been found out. They hadn't done anything with string anywhere, anytime in the building.

Everett took a deep breath, looked at Barbara and flung his open palms at Graham. "Aunt Barb, we have no idea what he's talking about."

He clearly couldn't turn his back on his role as spokesperson now whether he liked it or not. His authority, shaky as it was, let his younger brother know he would handle this unexpected and undeserved problem. For better or worse. As if in solidarity, Michael moved closer to Everett, and they stood together looking at Graham waiting for the next round of accusations.

"And sir," Everett continued then paused to look at his brother as if giving Michael one last chance to admit he alone was responsible, and getting no acknowledgment, continued, "I don't mean any disrespect if this was something you used to do when you were a kid but I, we, don't really see why someone would do something like that. It doesn't make any sense to me—to us—to tie string around people's doorknobs. How is that funny?"

Graham had to hand it to the kid. To respond so bravely and graciously to an adult's accusations was admirable. He was in an untenable position. They were good kids who could offer no proof that things were just fine between him and his wife; that she hadn't lied to her husband. So Graham did the only thing he could do. Let them off the hook as contritely and responsibly as possible.

"Boys," he said. "Barbara, I'm very sorry to have bothered you with what's obviously been a misunderstanding. Thank you all for talking with me and I'm sorry to have upset you since you had nothing to do with this." He again thrust his open palm with its wad of string toward them—the artificial evidence—to make his point. "Now that I think about it, the people I talked to weren't exactly sure that they'd seen you boys, and one of them has been confused in general about things lately." *Another lie, why not?* "I'm very sorry to say."

Everett looked at Michael, and with a single nod of his head, concluded he'd taken care of the matter, and that was that. Their standing their ground and the truth had set them free. And their honesty had helped reveal a fact they may not have known before: adults could be wrong.

"Well, I'm sorry, too," said Barbara. "I wish we could help shed some light on whoever is responsible for these antics. Boys, thank you for talking with Mr. Cavanaugh. Thank you for being honest."

"You're welcome," they said in unison. They looked at Graham with what he could only interpret as pity. It wasn't their fault he'd made a fool of himself, but they had both watched it happen.

"I'll leave you then," Graham said. "Thank you for your time and again, sorry about the misunderstanding. Such a minor thing anyway."

He took the stairs back to his floor, thinking about the irony of his final words to them. The explanation Joan had invented about the string, and, Graham was afraid, the presence of the string itself, were anything but minor.

For the next week he mentally rehearsed the imaginary conversation he never had with Joan because he could never get past his half of the discussion.

I want you to know I took care of that string business with Barbara's nephews, he replayed again and again. *You were right, Joan, they've been tying those strings on doorknobs for months. But it's over now and it won't happen again.*

Anticipating all the versions of her replies couldn't convince him that bringing it up would be a good idea. As time passed, and Joan's healthy pregnancy with Anne progressed, and Ceci became less of a baby and more of a little girl, and Graham became more confident and less worried about his performance in law school, and their marriage recovered from the rocky road it had detoured down, he believed more and more that never making that imaginary conversation a real one had been the right thing to do.

NEW CANAAN

1985

4

There was no scapegoat—real or imagined—to blame for Mark's death. And there was nothing sensational about what happened either. It had been, in the purest and saddest sense, a tragic accident.

Mark, Hutch's beautiful, thoughtful boy, who adored his mother. How he made her laugh with his imitations of the television characters from M*A*S*H. His best ones were Hawkeye and Winchester. The most gallant of all his friends toward girls, cutting loose a friend his sophomore year because of the cruel break-up the boy inflicted on the girl who lived next door to them. Mark, who managed to do just enough schoolwork, barely, to maintain a respectable GPA, then ace the final in every class and finish the year with nothing less than an A minus. Who was wearing his sweatshirt from Villanova when he died. Where he should have been a freshman that fall, and on the roster to play first base for the Wildcats.

Hutch supposed, of all people, the most likely one to blame would have been Mark himself for being in the wrong place at the wrong time. The universal equation of all tragedies.

Hutch tried to negotiate with God. *Please, if You don't let us lose him, I won't utter a single word of criticism, I'll only say, thank God you're all right, son. You're all right, that's all that matters.* When that didn't work, he imagined Mark coming back to life for just long enough for Hutch to unload his rage on him and God both: *Why the fuck were you riding in the back of a pick-up? What were you thinking?*

It was the night of their high school graduation and, although the other boys had been drinking, even drinking wasn't to blame. George Collins, who was driving, had type 1 diabetes. George never drank after the one time as a freshman when he ended up in the hospital, so he was always the one to drive the guys around on party nights. George was driving them—Mark, Scott Blakely and Nick Dawson, all varsity baseball players—home from a party at Rachel Morrison's. Scott was up in the cab with George, and Nick and Mark were riding in the open bed because they were getting dropped off first.

After they left Nick's house, a little after one in the morning, Mark was alone in the back when George took the turn on Silvermine Road. Maybe George was driving faster than he should have been, maybe the sliding back window was open, and all three boys were laughing—two on one side of the glass, one on the other—maybe the radio was playing loud, Dire Straits or David Bowie or Talking Heads, maybe Mark was doubled over laughing too hard to be hanging on— but none of that should have mattered. At the turn, George swerved to avoid the family of raccoons that darted into the beams of his headlights. He had veered toward the shoulder, wisely, but in doing so the truck's right back tire had skidded off the asphalt and onto the gravel slope, where the traction was unreliable, and which abutted a sharp drop-off into the woods. As the truck fishtailed, threatening to pull them off the road, George floored the gas, and Mark flew out of the truck and died on impact.

Of course, George shouldn't have been driving three other boys around in a truck that seated only one passenger safely, but people did it all the time back then, and no one considered it dangerous, the way they came to years later. And George's sister Stephanie, who was home for the summer from Middlebury, had taken the Collins's station wagon that night to drive her friends to another party. And the boys had done it before without incident, not frequently, but too many times to count, never for long distances, always only little jaunts around town.

Days later, sobbing on the couch in Hutch's living room with his face in his hands, George said to him, "We weren't even driving that far. Nick's house was only three miles from yours. I'm sorry. I'm so sorry!"

The only thing Hutch could do was hold the boy, whose shaking body was foreign for him to comfort—like and yet so unlike his lost child's—and murmur, "I know, son. I know."

He wouldn't have wished what George had to live with on anyone, and George shouldn't have had to bear it. He was the kid who had kept his high school friends safe because he had a disease that made drinking particularly threatening, so the rest of them were free to cut loose without a second thought, believing they could count on George to get them home.

5

After Mark died, Alice felt skinned, like a piece of fruit peeled by someone who was angry. Trying to move through the world in those first days and weeks, it was as though several layers of her skin, from the epidermis on down, had been stripped from her body. The feel of her own clothing hurt and even the air against her skin—this new sensitive inexplicable version of it—was its own assault. She thought of severely burned victims who survived fires only to face prolonged suffering as their organs failed and there was no chance of recovery. That tender, raw, charred skin beneath the sterile burn blankets that could only do so much until they were no longer needed. Only sleep brought relief and sometimes even in her dreams, when she had them, her skin ached.

And in those early weeks, when she shut down emotionally, and with Hutch entirely, she also felt like she should lock Julia in the basement and let her out only when Alice was on her own deathbed. The world was full of risks for one's children, and it was something Alice realized only after she had lost Mark. She had always been the parent when the kids were growing up who trusted everything would be okay, that *they* would be okay. She was not, back then, what they call today, *a helicopter parent.*

And the kids *were* okay, had been anyway. Despite choking hazards, falls out of bed and from jungle gyms, biking and skateboarding and skiing, Julia's riding lessons and

Mark's learning to drive with them after he got his permit, then driving by himself after he got his license. Surviving the parties kids had when parents were out of town. The flights they took together, the four of them flying on the same plane. All the trips to St. Bart's and Bermuda and the one to Italy, always giving the children a certain amount of freedom once they were old enough.

Now Alice didn't want Julia to learn to drive and after the funeral, when Julia asked to go stay with a friend, Alice was honestly relieved that in the short term she didn't have to try to be a good mother. What that would even have looked like, she had no idea.

Alice's mother Sarah came for the funeral and then stayed for a week, and Alice allowed herself to be taken care of like the child she felt like she had regressed into. Every night while Sarah was there, when she came in to say good night, Sarah held her while Alice sobbed and sobbed. And when her mother left after that week, Alice didn't know how to be with Hutch. It seemed to her like Mark's death had pulled loose a thread in their marriage, which then made all of the rest of it so easily unravel.

Of course there was Julia, her darling, but Mark was the child who had made them parents. Before that, they were just two married people, and with his death, the mortar binding them felt loose and flimsy and vulnerable. Alice knew it was one typical equation that made couples split—losing a child—and she could see why. Alice was the one who had always fixed everything for Hutch and Hutch was the one who had always fixed everything for Alice. Neither of them could fix this.

Their shared powerlessness could have united them in their grief, but Alice didn't want anything to do with anyone, including Hutch. Mark's death mocked and undermined the confidence she'd had in his safety his whole life. She hadn't only lost her son. Her unwavering confidence that her children would survive her had been shattered.

For a long time, Alice went to bed early. And on the tenderest nights, of which she lost count, she slept in Mark's room. There was no reason not to and after the first few months, when she finally started to feel like her skin, her own body, wasn't her enemy, it was the only respite she could get from the agony of every-day life, and its reality, but it was also the time, rarely, when she dreamt about Mark, and could be with him in that abstract and completely fabricated landscape and get some comfort that he was *okay*. And the dreams were so lovely! Then the morning would come and at first, for a few long seconds lying there, Alice would feel like she'd truly just visited him at college over the weekend and now having gotten back home, was waking up in her own bed—or Mark's—instead of a hotel.

And it wasn't like it had been in those days and early weeks when she opened her eyes for the first time and her cheeks were already wet from crying in her sleep. Instead, months later, the dreams left Alice with a lingering sense of happiness and peace and gratitude, both for the dream and for the life her son had and the friend he had been to Alice. The gift he'd been to all of them. The dreams were never elaborate and never had an identifiable setting, it was always just the two of them together, and Mark was smiling, and he was happy, and in Alice's dream-mind, whether she said it to him aloud or communicated to him silently, without words, the recurring message was always the same: *I miss you!*

There was one morning when she hadn't remembered dreaming of Mark that Hutch brought her coffee in bed and told Alice she'd been talking in her sleep.

"Do you remember anything from your dream last night?" he said. "Most of it was gibberish but at one point you said very clearly, 'Mark, please unload the dishwasher!' Then there was more gibberish."

Alice took the coffee from him. "Thank you for this," she said. She looked at him and smiled. "I have no recollection of that, but it sounds like something you'd overhear between the two of us, doesn't it? What was it like for you to hear that? Did it make you sad?"

That morning, Alice realized they were starting to find their ways back to each other from the first place they'd been: each dwelling in their own darkness; then the second: back to each other in grief and hopeless helplessness; and now finally, recognizing the friends they were to each other, in addition to being parents, spouses, lovers.

"No," Hutch said. "I wasn't sad. I actually laughed a little and felt a bit envious, honestly. If you were meeting up with him in a dream, I wish I could have joined you there, like walking into a different room from where I was to the one you both were in. And, since I couldn't do that, and I was awake, I lay there waiting for you to say something more, maybe to him. I felt a little bit like I was eavesdropping on someone else's conversation. But there wasn't anything else after the gibberish. You were quiet again, and very clearly asleep."

Alice hadn't told Hutch about her dreams about Mark, and that the chance of them, the hope for them, was one reason why she made a habit of going to bed early. There was no malice, Alice didn't think, in keeping all of that from Hutch, but deep down she feared that if she shared her dreams with him, and her motivations for her early bedtime, that it would jinx them from continuing to happen. Like literally bringing them into the light of day, sharing their existence with someone else—her husband, his father—would scare them away and encourage them to evaporate and disappear from Alice entirely. Although, if she was being honest, Alice felt proprietary about the dreams; if she and Hutch couldn't literally meet Mark together in real life, which they couldn't, something about them felt like hers and hers alone, not something for her to share with anyone else. But now, Alice thought this seemed like a good time to be generous.

"If I was dreaming about him, and the dishwasher, last night, I don't remember," she said. "But I have dreamt about him a few times." That quickly, opening up made her feel newly raw and sad. "Have you?"

"Just once that I remember," he said. He sighed and shook his head. "A few weeks after he died, I think. So strange. In the dream we had buried him but somehow he called me and told me we'd made a mistake, that he wasn't dead, and to go and dig up the casket and get him out. And we did, in that instant way things happen in dreams. We just went to the cemetery and opened the casket and he just got up and walked out. A relief, obviously, that we hadn't killed him by burying him alive. That's how I felt, so goddamn relieved, that he hadn't really died. But then I woke up. Maybe, if you've dreamt about him, too, you know what I mean."

"I do, Hutch," Alice said. "I do know what you mean."

For several minutes they sat there in silence, drinking their coffee, wiping their eyes.

After that morning, Alice started staying up later. She realized her early bedtime was built on a fallacy: the chance for her to chase a ghost, and the existence of a make-believe portal where she might find him. But in the light of day, talking to her husband, the two of them crying together, Alice realized, and maybe Hutch did, too, their dreams were merely the products of their reeling minds, alternately seeking to heal and yet resisting, bitterly, the process of letting go, moving on and recovering from what had been taken from them.

6

Being in her own house was so unbearable that Julia spent most of that summer at her friend Lauren's. Because she practically moved in with Lauren's family for several weeks, it was like her parents became childless again. Whether that worsened or aided their surviving Mark's death, individually and together, Julia had no idea. Without her to consider, Hutch and Alice could have come together and prevailed as a couple, or each retreated to their own corners and mourned alone, becoming more alienated from each other in the process. She only thought about that later. At the time she just wanted to not be a member of her family, at least for a little while. Julia was alternately heartbroken and numb, either weeping to the point of exhaustion or silent for hours, but it was agonizing to be the object of so many people's condolences and pity and sad attention. She was the sophomore girl whose brother had died the night of his high school graduation. That's what she was known for.

Lauren wasn't her best friend; her best friend Tara was the catalyst to bring them together when they were freshmen, but Tara's family spent every summer in Sag Harbor. A friendship triangle can be challenging, but the relationship between the three of them had always been formulaic, eliminating any conflict: Julia as Tara's first choice, Lauren as her number two, and as far as Lauren and Julia were concerned, they hit it off when the three of them did something together, which had been the only occasions Julia and Lauren spent time with each other. Part of the reason that dynamic worked for Julia was because Lauren was never a threat to her friendship with Tara, so she could afford to be big-hearted when their pair expanded into three.

Tara was Julia's constant companion the week after Mark's death, was by her side at the funeral and cemetery and reception, and without asking either set of parents—Tara just told hers what she was doing—slept five nights in a row at Julia's house after Mark died. After the funeral, Tara went home before her family left for Sag Harbor, and then she was gone until just before Labor Day.

That same week Julia's grandmothers and grandfathers and aunts and uncles from both sides of the family descended upon their house and took over. Her mother seemed to shrink physically, because of her grief, but also because of how large everyone who came to help loomed in comparison with their hushed but confident voices wielding authority and protection, answering the phone and making calls, delaying visitors. Arranging casseroles in the refrigerator to be eaten on an upcoming night of the week or dated and frozen for a later time. Moving flowers from one room to another, or to a different table, until one morning Alice took every arrangement—vases and foliage alike, still green and fresh enough for days to come—and threw them in their curbside trashcan, one after another, making trip after trip in and out through the front door until they were all gone.

No one tried to stop her. No one even said anything. Everyone just stayed out of her way. Hutch became defensive and argumentative in response to people attempting to help and take responsibilities off his hands. The company and their good intentions made the house feel congested and contentious. There was no right way to do anything.

A week after Mark's funeral, Hutch got into a shouting match with Alice's father, Jim. Alice's parents had stayed on, long after all the other relatives left and went home, and two days longer than Hutch's parents. That morning Jim was sitting with Julia in the kitchen, drinking coffee, and they both saw her father take the lawnmower out of the shed. Her grandfather walked out to the yard and put his hand on Hutch's shoulder. Julia was eating toast and reading a book, and because the window was open—and since her father was shouting—she heard some of their conversation but not all of it. Her mother was still in bed, which she had been for most of the day, every day that week.

Julia didn't hear what her grandfather first said to her father. He had a quiet, steady voice even up close, but he kept his hand on Hutch's shoulder and her father kept his hands on the handle of the lawnmower. For a minute or two her grandfather nodded, *Yes*, and her father shook his head, *No*, and their responses turned into a mesmerizing pattern that Julia couldn't look away from even though the only things moving were her grandfather's mouth and both of their heads until her father stepped out and away from her grandfather's hand on his shoulder and said, "Jesus Christ, Jim, my son is dead, but I can mow my own fucking lawn. Go light a candle somewhere. Or better yet just go home."

Jim was a sensible man who respected Hutch, so he did the only thing he could which was leave her broken father to mow his own lawn. Her grandfather came back into the kitchen, kissed Julia on the head, and he and her grandmother packed and went back to Philadelphia that day.

Then it was just the three of them. During the short time when their house was full, Julia had figured out this much: When someone dies, though people mean well, they can't entirely avoid doing the wrong thing.

A week after Tara and her family left for Sag Harbor, Lauren called and asked if Julia wanted to spend the night.

"It's okay if you don't want to," Lauren said. "You won't hurt my feelings. I just thought you might want to get out of your house for a little while. It's all I could think of to try and help."

Julia couldn't think of the last time she'd been so grateful for a genuine gesture of kindness, and it wasn't lost on her that Lauren took a risk extending herself the way she did. Lauren didn't know Julia so well that she could have anticipated her response, and without Tara around to act as a liaison, or weigh in, or be Julia's primary source of comfort, Lauren's invitation made her vulnerable to whatever line of fire Julia's grief could have caught her in.

Julia didn't even hesitate to respond. "Yes," she said. "Thank you. Oh, my God, I need a break from this place. I'm so glad you called."

"My mom and I will come pick you up," she said. "Just tell me when."

Lauren hadn't known Mark well, and not the way Tara did. Tara and Mark had had their own friendship. As Julia's best friend, she was both an extension of her, and someone Mark had to treat better than his sister. So until she'd left for Sag Harbor, Tara's grief was closer to Julia's than it wasn't. One of three girls in her own family, she had signed his yearbook: *To my 'big brother' Mark, Stay awesome 4 ever! Love always, Your other 'little sis!'—T*

While Julia was grateful for Lauren's invitation, she also wasn't sure how it would pan out. All she knew was that she needed an emergency escape from her family—such as it now was—and Lauren had provided one. Julia was confident the unknown couldn't be any worse than staying home.

After Lauren and her mother came by, and her mother and Julia's mother spoke for a few minutes—Lauren's mother had brought a quiche and two loaves of banana bread—they drove back to her house, where Julia had never been before. Whenever the three of them had spent time together, it had always been at Tara's. Lauren lived with her parents and younger brother Jack, who was twelve. After they put Julia's stuff in her room, they took her dog, Barnacle, for a walk.

"His real name is Barney," Lauren said, as if Julia had asked. "But we never call him that. He's always right on top of you, you know, like attached, like a barnacle. You want a cigarette?" She pulled two out of her jacket pocket and offered one to Julia. "My mom sneaks them, and I sneak them from her," she said. "I don't smoke a lot or anything. I'm glad you came over."

Julia took a cigarette. She, Tara and Lauren had never smoked together, and Julia only ever tried it once with one of her older cousins the previous summer on the Fourth of July. "Me, too," she said.

"My real dad died when I was three and Jack was a baby," Lauren said. "My dad now is really my stepdad. I don't remember a lot about my real dad. He was a policeman and was shot one night by someone he pulled over. We lived in Virginia then. We moved to Connecticut when I was five after my mom got remarried."

"I didn't know that," Julia said. "God. I'm really sorry."

"I don't tell a lot of people," she said. "It's not anything they need to know but I thought you should."

They walked Barnacle and smoked their cigarettes and that was the beginning of how Julia survived the first summer without her brother, without the help of her parents, and mostly in Lauren's house.

NEW YORK

1988

7

Periodically, for as long as she could remember, Anne fantasized about living with another family. There was never anything specific about these imaginary people; it was simply a different household that in her mind she would walk into, having always already spiritually existed there, but only finally moved in. She wondered if it was because she was the middle child. She was independent and sometimes felt like she was the last of her sisters to be considered or consulted by their parents, but it didn't happen all the time and when she felt sensitive about it, her emotions made her feel needy and weak, which she was determined not to be. The inexplicable loneliness she didn't understand wasn't always there, but whenever it abated, Anne knew it would be back.

She loved her parents and her sisters, but when they were kids, Ceci acknowledged her only when it suited her, and Carolyn always seemed above reproach and had more friends than seemed fair. In middle school, Anne came up with an experiment to challenge her visibility: she started swearing around her family. The result was unexpected but not surprising: her mother made it a lesson about manners. But since she didn't outright forbid it at home, Anne felt like the experiment had failed—she was no longer interested in profanity.

There were ebbs and flows of the pull toward the *other* family. She wondered what it would be like to be one of the kids of two beloved teachers, one in elementary school, years later, one in high school. Another benefit of the dream of living with her high school cross country coach, a powerful and influential woman, and her husband and young son, was the possibility of becoming her top runner—Anne was always the sixth girl on the team. In college, she imagined moving in with either of the families of her two closest friends, both of whom she spent a lot of time with, although the draw of the *other* family had weakened by then.

But when Anne spent her junior year abroad in Italy and fell in love with Peter Herring, another student at their college whose path had never crossed hers until they were abroad, *that* combination felt like the solution she had been seeking and imagining in the *other* family all those years—feeling like her truest self in a foreign country and being with someone who truly saw her, loved her, wanted to marry her. After graduation Anne got a job at a magazine in Italy and returned to work there, but by then she had ended her relationship with Peter and terminated their unplanned pregnancy. She knew all too well of her mother's becoming a parent so young and her limited choices because of it, and Anne didn't want to repeat the legacy.

She would do, and be, something different.

★ ★ ★

One afternoon, when Anne had been back from Italy for more than a month, she and Joan went for a walk in Central Park. Her mother was having a good day, the sun was out, it was almost Thanksgiving and the air smelled like the season.

In early October, Joan's oncologist had called Anne at work and told her that Joan might have just six months. Anne had said, *My mother didn't tell me that, why are you telling me that?* And the doctor said, *Because you live in Italy.*

Weeks later the company that owned the magazine where she worked found her a desk in New York.

They were walking toward Woolman Rink and Joan said, "Oh, Anne, we should go skating! Don't you think? All of us together. Wouldn't that be fun?" She clapped her hands.

"We'll see, Mom," said Anne. "Maybe. We should probably discuss if that's a good idea for you."

"For God's sake if I can walk, I can skate," Joan said. "There's not much to discuss."

From the other direction a family was walking toward them: a mother and father and their two children, who looked close in age, both between two and three. The kids both sported long hair so it was unclear if they were boys or girls. Each child was wearing what looked like a harness, and each adult was connected to one of the children with a leash that was attached to the wristbands both parents wore.

"Oh, for Christ's sake," Joan said. "Will you look at that. Why are these people even in the park with their children on leashes like dogs? They don't think they could catch them if the kids took off?"

"Mom," said Anne. "You don't know what their story is. People are strange. Maybe they had a scare once. Who knows?"

Although Anne had only been home since just before Halloween, occasionally she had noticed a difference in her mother; everyone knew the cancer had spread to her brain, and Joan was mostly the same, most of the time, but when she wasn't herself, infrequently, it was because an uncharacteristic deep-seated rage reared its head and out of nowhere, emerged from her.

The family walked closer and as they did Anne could see Joan scrutinizing the dynamic among the four of them, getting ready—maybe, or maybe not—to give them a piece of her mind, and a deluge of criticism and possibly anger they didn't deserve. And, in trying to interpret what her mother was seeing, Anne looked at the family closely herself.

It did seem, Anne thought, like the couple—except for the existence of the hardware of the harnesses—was tuning out both children. They seemed to be arguing and each of them, with the hand that wasn't attached to the leash and the kid, was gesticulating. *They look like dysfunctional parental bookends*, Anne thought.

"Look at them," said Joan. "They have those kids tethered so they can argue without paying attention to them. It's disgusting." She looked at Anne. "I have to say something."

"No, Mom, you actually don't," said Anne. "Let's keep going on our way and let them go on theirs. It's a free country, this is a public park, and the world is full of weirdos. We're in New York."

"I do," said Joan. "I have to say something. For all the people who've seen them and are thinking the same thing and didn't speak up, I will. This isn't something I'm going to ignore or walk away from. Choices have consequences Anne. And people have eyes."

The couple—the man and the woman—weren't young, late thirties maybe, Anne thought, and as much as she didn't want the crazy dustup that Joan was going to initiate, she did agree with her mother. Who the fuck took kids to Central Park to walk them on a harness like a dog who might bolt?

The couple got closer, and Joan waved her hand at them like she was walking toward someone picking her up from the airport and greeting them from a distance.

She stepped out in front of them. "Hello, hello!" Joan said. "Pardon me for a moment."

The couple stopped and their leashed children stopped, too.

"Is this your first time visiting the city?" Joan said. She smiled at the couple and looked down at the children and smiled at them. She clasped her hands together. "How wonderful."

The man and woman looked at each other. They looked at Joan and at Anne. Anne watched all of it wondering what was going to happen next.

The man looked alternately surprised and irritated. "Excuse me?"

And before her eyes, Anne saw her mother undergo a transformation and become an aggressive, cruel person she didn't recognize.

"I can't imagine why you have your children chained up like prison inmates picking up garbage along the side of the road." Joan said. "The only thing I can think of is you're unbearably skittish about being in the city for the first time. That, or you have to be attached to them so you can fight undisturbed."

The woman spoke, her mouth tight. "We're visiting his sister and brother-in-law for Thanksgiving. Small place, lots of family, several little ones. I'm sure you can imagine."

"Janet," the man said, with a look at his wife that silenced her. Then he turned back to Joan. "I don't know who the fuck you think you are lady, and I don't give a shit. Fuck off." He turned on his heel, and with his free hand against the small of his wife's back, guided her to do the same and the family walked away from Anne and Joan, the children trailing their parents.

"You fuck off!" Joan called after them.

And Anne thought, *Dear God, where is my mother?*

People walking by who had seen and heard the exchange were now stopping and turning their heads to alternately stare at Joan, and Anne, and the retreating family. New Yorkers shouting at each other right here in Central Park!

That quickly, Joan newly appeared small, frightened and confused as to what she'd just been a part of, and tears streamed down her face.

"Oh, Anne, I'm sorry. I didn't think, I didn't mean to do that. I'm so sorry."

Anne put her arm around her mother's shoulder, and steered her back the way they came, retracing their steps back out of the park. "I know, it's okay," she said. "That guy was an asshole. You were just concerned. Let's get home and have a cup of tea. Maybe you feel like lying down."

Joan brightened. "Yes, yes. I was concerned. No child should be treated that way, certainly no good parent would do such a thing. Maybe if they hadn't already been fighting with each other he would have understood what I was saying, don't you think? But a cup of tea and a little lie-down sound lovely. Anne, don't worry, everything is going to be okay."

And Anne thought, *This is no way to live. How much worse is this going to get?*

8

Christmas night, after the table was cleared, Joan asked Ceci if they could talk, just the two of them, and they sat in the living room admiring the tree, sipping red wine. Ceci's ten-month-old son, Wyatt, lay on the floor next to the couch under a baby play gym kicking and cooing at the elephant, zebra, giraffe and mirror hanging from the intersecting arches above him.

"You outdid yourself, again, Mom. Dinner was fabulous," Ceci lifted her glass and tapped it against Joan's. "Merry Christmas."

"It really was, wasn't it? But it was a group effort. I certainly could not have pulled that off by myself," Joan said. "Thanks for all your help, sweetheart." Joan patted Ceci's hand. "You are always such a big help, even when you have your own hands full."

"I didn't do more than anyone else tonight, but thanks," Ceci said. "We're all happy to step up. You must know that. Carolyn and Anne both have been doing far more than I have."

"Oh, I know, love," Joan sighed. "I know all that. But John is busy with work and traveling with a baby is never easy. If you were another type of person, you could easily leverage all that to get out of jail free."

"Okay, Mom," Ceci laughed. "But come on, being here for Christmas together, helping to serve, and enjoy, a lovely dinner is hardly a prison sentence."

"I just love you sweetie," said Joan. "So much. And I have to tell you I'm confident we won't all be doing this together again next year."

"Oh, Mom," said Ceci. "Come on. Please don't. You don't know what's going to happen."

"Well, you're right," Joan said. "I can't predict the future, but I have a sense of what's going on in my own body and I have a doctor who's honest with me. And I'd rather have this conversation with you, as difficult as it may be, than regret that I didn't once it's too late. You can be sad. I'm sad, too."

Ceci put down her wine glass and picked up Joan's left hand and held it between both of hers.

"You're such a good mother, sweetie," Joan turned and looked at Wyatt. "You've really done a good job and I'm so proud of you. He's so happy, that's how you can tell. You know I look at him and I can remember you at exactly the same age. You're doing a much better job than I did.

"And I want you to remember that when the time comes, you're going to have to be in charge a little bit. You're the oldest, and whether you like it or not Anne and Carolyn are going to need someone to take the lead, just provide a little direction, so much so that they might not even realize you're doing the thing they need. When the time comes, you'll know what I mean. It's not going to be all that much different from having been the oldest your whole life," Joan laughed.

"So I'm not telling you anything you don't already know, it will just be different when I'm not here anymore and it will just be the three of you and Dad."

"Okay," Ceci said. "I think we've all thought that we'll just figure it out. When that time comes, whenever that may be. You could be wrong, Mom, I'm just saying."

Ceci wasn't entirely shocked that they were having this conversation, but Joan's bluntness, and how directly she brought it up, were still unexpected. Yet, no matter when it was going to take place, or how her mother might broach the painful subject of her death and its aftermath, it wasn't ever going to be an exchange Ceci was comfortable having.

"I'm not asking you to do anything that you wouldn't normally, or naturally," Joan said. "I just want to be clear. There won't be very much to figure out, and Dad and I have gotten our affairs in order. Isn't that such a strange expression?"

Joan started to laugh and then couldn't stop. For almost a minute Ceci waited for her to stop and continue talking.

"I'm sorry, I just got the giggles," Joan finally said and wiped her eyes. "But what a strange phrase. My word. It sounds like, 'Make sure all the affairs you've been having are in order before you die,' doesn't it? Why not just say arrangements?

"Anyway, all the details that need to be finalized have been and that's something that's important to me, and to your dad, but I'm talking about something else. I just want to make sure—for you to remind everyone if it's necessary—how much I love you all. Especially Carolyn, because of how prickly I know I can be with her, and especially Anne, for different reasons."

"Mom, I know, we know," said Ceci. "I will of course in the extraordinary unlikelihood that that will ever be necessary. I think you're feeling the wine and that's okay. But I think you're inventing things a little bit."

"You can think what you want Ceci, but this has nothing to do with me being a little tipsy, believe me. But this is why I'm asking for your help, sweetheart," said Joan. "I know over the years of the three of you I have been harder on Anne than you and Carolyn and it's complicated, to be both proud and resentful that she has found happiness that doesn't include her family, in another country, so far away from us. I don't ever want her to think that I didn't support her doing exactly what she wanted."

"Okay, Mom," Ceci said. "Why don't we think about calling it a night? Or find something good on TV. Let's see what everyone else is doing."

"Fine. Maybe you think I'm being strange or melodramatic or maudlin or who knows what," said Joan. "But when this little guy—" she reached down and squeezed Wyatt's foot— "is a teenager, and then a college graduate, and has become his own person, believe me, you'll look back and hope you did things right more than you didn't. And then maybe you'll also remember the time we had this uncomfortable talk on Christmas night that made you think I was a little crazy."

Joan set down her glass and put her arms around Ceci and pulled her toward her.

"And I'm sorry when that time comes that I won't be here to tell you, yes, Ceci, you did more things right than you didn't, and what a good mother you've been," Joan said. "Just like I have tonight."

NEW YORK

1989

9

Four days after Joan's funeral, on April first, it had officially been spring for almost two weeks, but the morning dawned with rain that lasted all day, punishing the shocked and optimistic crocuses and tulips that had dared to bloom, and belying that just two days earlier the temperature had reached seventy degrees. The weather contributed an additional layer of gloom to the task that lay ahead of Anne, Carolyn and Ceci: going through Joan's jewelry. It wasn't something that was pressing or had to be done today, but it was Graham who had insisted on it, gently.

Ceci and her family had to get back to Boston, and Anne was returning to Italy in a matter of weeks. It felt important to Graham, he told them, to have the jewelry matter wrapped up. He choked up when he told them what he needed them to do. With it all still there waiting for her to wear, he said, for just a few seconds every morning he was deceived into thinking that maybe she wasn't gone. Her jewelry, more than even her clothing, was the emotional symbol of Joan's presence. Her clothes would be dealt with in time, after the girls had taken the nicest pieces they each wanted, cashmere wraps and sweaters, a shell and cardigan set, a camel hair coat. But the rings, and bangles, cuff bracelets, earrings, and chunky necklaces still on display, or in the jewelry boxes on her dressing table continued to imply some suggestion of her imminent appearance.

It was part of Graham's ask when he told them, "On the bright side, it's the worst thing you'll do all day."

So at eleven o'clock that morning, with a cold bottle of Sauvignon Blanc, they brought Joan's three jewelry boxes, ring holder and necklace tree and began laying out the pieces on the dining room table. In one of the jewelry boxes there was a note from Joan addressed to Peter Herring, Anne's old boyfriend, that Anne put in her room.

Then, they decided, first, that each of them would take back for themselves anything they had given Joan. Ceci had given her the most, two necklaces and an exquisite David Yurman bracelet; Anne had given her a silver, monogrammed Tiffany cuff and a pair of mixed metal dangling earrings. Carolyn had given Joan a necklace with a sage-green glass pendant from a boutique in SoHo for Mother's Day the previous year, which none of them had known would be Joan's last Mother's Day.

Then they laid out all the pieces that Graham had given her over the years or that Joan had bought herself. This was the part that took the longest and was the saddest, and Anne asked him to come and see if there was anything he wanted to keep. "Anything at all, for any reason," she said. "We've all agreed."

Graham did as they asked, looked over the lifetime of gifts he'd given her, and the pieces she had treasured and had picked to define her, wiped his eyes and said, no, he didn't. The only things he wanted to keep were her wedding band and engagement ring, which he had taken out of the jewelry boxes before the girls got started. After the viewing, before the casket was closed, the night before the funeral, he had taken off his wedding ring and put it on Joan's left ring finger. That was the only jewelry she'd been buried with.

It took a little over an hour and they cried and laughed and remembered her favorite pieces and their memories of her wearing them. The only contention arose from a pair of bronze earrings Joan had gotten in Spain during the summer five years earlier, the last trip abroad they'd taken as a family. They were Carolyn's favorite, but Anne claimed that taking them back to Italy with her would be like taking a piece of Joan back with her to her home there, and the earrings closer to their place of origin.

From time to time, not frequently but not rarely either, there had been tension brewing, bordering on arguments, enough times over the previous months between Anne and Carolyn about who was doing more, about whose sacrifice had been greater to be caring for their mother. Carolyn contested that her leaving school, compared with Anne's leaving her life and job in Italy was the far greater disruption. Anne claimed her decision had more significant consequences challenging to bounce back from. Every time it came up, after a comment under someone's breath or a resentful posture, they skirted the issue; neither of them wanted to have a debate over a matter so delicate and inarguable as caring for their dying mother. Since they'd both made their decisions, obviously without hesitation when they realized what had been necessary, it was an appalling issue to make comparisons about.

So in the end, Carolyn relented and said Anne should take the bronze earrings from Spain, a gesture, which, when Anne realized was the more selfless position, then declined, insisting that Carolyn should keep them.

"I know what you're doing," said Anne. "And I'm not going to let you give up something you love so much."

"Really?" Carolyn said. "Or you just refuse to let me be the more generous person? That's really what's going on here. Seriously, Anne, just take them for God's sake."

"This is happening right now, over our mother's—who we have just buried—jewelry?" said Anne. "Nice."

And Ceci said, "Come on, you guys. Please don't."

So that afternoon Carolyn agreed to take the earrings, and two weeks after Anne returned to Italy, she received a package from Carolyn with the earrings and a note: *Enjoy. I'll borrow them the next time you're home. Xoxo—C*

After that, Anne didn't speak to Carolyn for three months. And when they saw each other a year and a half later, at Christmas, neither of them mentioned the earrings, and by then, Anne didn't have them anymore. Three days after she'd gotten Carolyn's package, Anne wore the earrings when she went out with friends, got drunk and went home with a guy she met at a bar near the Piazza Navona. The next morning before she left his apartment, she intentionally left the earrings on the counter next to his bathroom sink and never saw him, or the earrings again.

10

After Ceci, John and Wyatt went back to Boston, Carolyn, Anne and Graham lived in a world that didn't extend beyond the apartment. Friends called, left messages, asked to come by, leaving the three of them to try and adjust to the new normal. For Carolyn, that new normal was staying in the same clothes for days straight without showering, ordering in Chinese food for them every night whether their father and Anne wanted it or not. The fridge was full of cartons of what they hadn't eaten or never opened.

It wasn't like Carolyn to be such a slob, but she was so exhausted and heartbroken she couldn't be bothered. Subconsciously her slovenliness was a tool she used to will her mother to walk in and show them all how to shape up. And since it was April, there was no way she could return to school even if she'd wanted to, and she didn't.

Carolyn didn't know how she and Anne and their father passed all those days. But one day stood out: Anne came into her room and sat on her bed and told Carolyn she was booking a flight back to Italy in the next week or two, she was still deciding. The magazine Anne worked for had arranged for a temporary assignment in one of the parent company's other offices where she'd been working since she'd come back to New York last fall, and it had never been a question of if she'd go back to Italy, but when.

Carolyn envied Anne; that she had something to return to, a job that had let her know she was worth waiting for, the chance to be in a different country, and that those things offered her a distraction from what she'd gone through the previous months. Carolyn had none of those things. She had finished the first semester of her freshman year of college and decided not to go back after the Christmas break. And now her mother was gone, and Carolyn had nothing.

"Why don't you come with me?" Anne said that day in Carolyn's room. "If you can't start school again until the fall, what else are you going to do?"

"I can't leave Dad," Carolyn said. "That would be a horrible thing to do to him. I'll find a job somewhere. I'll go back to Macy's. They'll hire me back." She had worked there the past three summers in the bed and bath department.

"Carolyn, Dad's known for a long time this was coming," Anne said. "You've already taken enough time out of your own life. He knows that, too. Any day now I bet you anything he's going to be asking you what you're going to do too, and he's not going to have you here being his roommate on the list of options. I'm sure he'd think your coming with me is a good idea. You can always wait a few weeks and come then. Think about it. It's a long time until school starts again in the fall."

Carolyn knew she was right, or partially right, but after Anne left she burrowed in her bed and cried until she fell asleep.

Their mother's four sisters, their four aunts, were another matter. Their mother was the middle of five girls: Celeste, Margaret, Joan, Bridget and Jacqueline. Until Anne went back to Italy and Graham returned to work, the aunts rotated days and shifts and meals like interchangeable school principals or head nurses on a ward where patients had been, and would be, for a long time. Carolyn knew it wasn't just for Joan's family, it was for the aunts, too, that they had the grieving family to dote on, keep busy, make sure they stayed intact. All the aunts' families took care of themselves while Joan's sisters came to fill the absence that she had left.

In the beginning Carolyn hadn't even known her aunts were there. The day after the funeral when she slept until two in the afternoon, she was surprised to see Celeste in the living room doing needlepoint, listening to public radio, the volume very low, barely audible.

Without looking up from her work, Celeste said, "Hi, sweetheart, can I make you something to eat? There's still so much food that people have brought. How did you sleep?"

It may as well have been nine o'clock on a Saturday morning when Carolyn was a fifth grader and Celeste had stayed with the girls when their parents went to England and Ireland for two weeks, for the matter-of-fact way she asked her those questions. But there was no place or need for melodrama at that point, for as bereaved as they all were and just as she had years ago, Celeste's offer said much more than the words themselves: *I'm here to take care of you since your mother's gone. Tell me what you need.*

The aunts were all different. Celeste, being the oldest, most easily assumed the role of authority even in a house that wasn't her own, with the expectation that everyone else accepted her authority just as easily.

Bridget and Jacqueline most often came together. The closest to each other in age—just thirteen months apart—for most of their lives they had been more like one unit made of two parts than two individuals. They reminded Carolyn of a married couple—although they were each married to their own husbands—for how consistently they seemed to know how best to work together without much if any discussion.

The days they were with them in the apartment, Bridget made a lot of phone calls and Jacqueline took care of the house, encouraged Carolyn to shower, asked for her help in cooking meals that they all ate together instead of ordering take-out.

The two of them, more than Celeste and Margaret when they came, offered almost a kind of entertainment—like Carolyn's daytime movies or TV at night with her father. They always had a lot to talk about with each other, included Carolyn in conversations they were having, asking her questions to get as much engagement as they could out of her. It wasn't gratuitous either, or patronizing; they were just very good, the two of them together, at providing an alternative activity to what was really going on.

Margaret was the aunt whose days with them Carolyn least looked forward to. She was the sister who most closely resembled Joan—and she knew it—so the days she was with them were full of cruel tricks as Carolyn passed by a room, saw Margaret out of the corner of her eye and imagined it was her mother. And because of their resemblance, Margaret's attitude during the days she was with them seemed like a combination of guilt and overcompensation, both for not being Joan, and for still being alive.

After Anne returned to Italy and Carolyn started showering again, Graham threw himself back into his work. He had been given as much flexibility as he'd wanted from his partners as Joan's illness worsened leading up to the end and even after she died, the partners were still telling Graham to take as much time as he needed, that they had things covered, clients were happy, everything was under control.

But her father discovered, as most people in his situation did, that there was no better distraction from a painful loss than work. So weeks after her mother's funeral, her father was out of the house by seven o'clock at the latest every morning and, most days, didn't return home until seven or eight that night. Even on weekends he went in for four or five hours during the day. When Graham came home, the two of them watched TV with takeout food and their drinks—white wine for Carolyn, bourbon for him, until it reached a reasonable hour to call it a night.

It hadn't occurred to Carolyn while her mother was still alive, but she and her father had been cohorts in her care and in charge of normalizing as much as they could for her and everyone else. And now, with her mother gone, she and her father still seemed like two soldiers, ready to be united in combat every day but there was no battle to wage, no reconnaissance to plan. There were just hours to get through, eating, drinking, sleeping, working, living, such as they were.

With her father gone long hours at the office, Carolyn had to find something to do. Although she told Anne she would, she didn't check to see if Macy's would hire her back. There was something about the idea of returning to a job she'd had when her mother was alive and well—when she would come in to shop and take Carolyn to lunch on her break—made it one she couldn't return to. The store would be exactly the same and she was not.

While she decided what to do, Carolyn went to the movies every day until she'd seen everything that was playing in theaters. The daytime was the worst part, when she was alone after her father had left for the day, when she imagined what her friends at college were doing—going to class, skipping class, studying, having sex, partying, meeting for lunch—and movies made the days easier to get through. If she could, she'd walk to the theater where whatever she wanted to see was showing since walking also took time so between sleeping in, cleaning the kitchen and doing laundry, walking to the movies, sitting in the theater and walking home and thinking about what to order in, Carolyn was able to get through one day at a time. Then the nights with her father and their TV and their drinks were the rewards for putting another day behind them.

Carolyn's best friend from college and her best friend from high school both called as regularly as they could, and they sent letters letting her know they were thinking of her, worrying about her, wondering how she was, wondering what she would do next. Every time Carolyn's answer was the same: *I haven't figured it out yet. What are you up to?* She guessed that's one reason why the calls and letters got more and more infrequent as the weeks and months passed.

A Barnes and Noble had recently opened on 86th, so one Monday afternoon on the way to the movies, Carolyn stopped there and filled out a job application while she had a cup of coffee and a croissant in the café. When she completed it and returned it to the guy at the information desk, he took the application without looking at her and it disappeared down behind the counter where he was standing.

"They're not hiring right now, but if anything opens up and they want to talk to you, they'll give you a call." He was reading the sports page of the *Daily News* folded open in front of him.

"Do you like working here?" Carolyn asked. She guessed he was a few years older than she was.

He looked up at her, seeing her for the first time. "More than I like not having a job," he said. "But it's not like I'm hoping to work up the ladder and become the manager one day. It's not like my quality of life is improving every day I work here."

"What a ringing endorsement," Carolyn said. "But you're getting paid to read the paper, right?" She pointed at what he was reading. "So there's that. Maybe you should read the *Times* instead. That might improve your quality of life."

He looked at her, and down at his paper, and reached under to where he'd put her application and laid it on the counter next to the newspaper.

"So, Carolyn," he said. He scanned the first page and turned it over and read the back. "Why do you want to join the team at Barnes and Noble? Why aren't you back at school?"

Before she could answer with her honest reason, which she'd written on the application in response to the very question the guy just asked, he read her answer.

"Oh, man," he said. "I'm really sorry. I don't know what to say. That's really awful. I'm so sorry. And sorry I was an asshole."

"Is your default to be an asshole unless you're talking to someone whose mother has died?"

He looked embarrassed and ashamed. "No," he said. "It's not. It's just that working retail is kind of a drag sometimes and I really didn't want to be bothered but you kept talking. I'm sorry about that, too."

"You could make it up to me," Carolyn said.

He smiled and looked unsure about what she would say next. The whole time they'd been talking he looked less and less comfortable about what was going to come out of her mouth next. "Okay," he said.

"You could take my application to your boss or manager or whoever and tell them they should hire me," Carolyn said. "I'll wait. I don't have anywhere else to go right now except the movies."

He stared at Carolyn for a few long seconds, and she could see him deciding what to say to her, and what to do next.

"I'm Nate, by the way," he said. "It's nice to meet you." He extended his hand, and Carolyn shook it. "And just so you know, it's not a bad place to work, really. I'll be right back, if you want to wait in the café."

"Sure," she said. "I was just there. I'm happy to go back. Thanks."

"The manager's name is Rob," Nate said. "He's a cool guy. I'll see if he's free. Good luck."

And after talking to Rob for almost forty-five minutes, while Nate walked by more than once, sometimes with a customer, sometimes by himself, Carolyn had accepted a job offer and had agreed to start two days later.

After she and Rob shook hands, Carolyn went back to the information desk, but Nate was gone, having been replaced by two women, both older than her. When they asked if she needed help, she asked if they could tell her where Nate was and they both peered at the schedule under a piece of glass on top of the wood and said together, "Register."

He was ringing up a customer with a toddler as Carolyn walked by, putting one book after another into a handled shopping bag, and called out to her over the woman's head.

"Hey, how did it go?" he said.

"We're going to be working together. See you Wednesday."

"Cool," he said. "See you then."

"Hey, and thanks," Carolyn added.

"You bet," he said, and continued ringing up the woman with the toddler.

Carolyn walked out of the store and as soon as she was outside and walking south on Lexington, she started to cry. This was her going on with her life without her mother and without her aunts, getting a new job without her father's help, and making a friend.

PORTLAND

2001

11

In late June, Carolyn was still pregnant with the girls when their next-door neighbor Frances moved to Holladay Park Plaza, a retirement community where she'd been on the waiting list for two years, and she and her son put her house on the market. The house had good bones but needed work, so it was impossible to predict how long before it sold. In a few months the whole world would change, and never be the same, but the housing market was still years from the brink of crisis.

Carolyn watched the real estate agents and their clients coming and going during the week, if she was home, and on the weekends, from various vantage points—the kitchen window, the front porch, the upstairs landing, the back patio. She watched strangers pull up and park, look the house and street up and down—some squinting, some frowning, many smiling or expressionless—talk among themselves, climb the front steps and disappear inside, reappear outside and circle the exterior, survey the backyard, then turn and look north and scrutinize her house.

Spying like the nosy neighbor in a sitcom, every time she saw a potential buyer arrive, she tried as best she could—from the unreliable distance of her home—to guess who would be pleasant to live next to and who they'd have to tolerate. Frances had been a good neighbor for two years, since Carolyn and Palmer bought their house in 1999, and because she had macular degeneration and no longer drove, the driveway they shared hadn't been an issue. But invariably at some point during their tour of the house, the agents and their clients ended up on Frances's side, cocking their heads, looking curious and uncertain, crossing their arms while they gazed toward Carolyn's house and the single driveway—the width of only one car—that led from the street to two parallel parking slabs, twice the width of the driveway, one for one of their cars—usually Carolyn's—one for whoever would buy Frances's house.

The configuration exuded a certain quaint and intimate charm, since although there was ultimately enough room for two cars to park side by side in front of the two garages, the driveway was only wide enough for one car at a time to pull in or back out, much like the way the two arms of a capital 'Y' converge into a singular vertical stem. A potential inconvenience in the millennium, the driveway was a testament to a simpler time in the Alameda neighborhood of northeast Portland, 1919, the year both houses were built, when a driveway of that proportion must have been a luxury.

They could be juggling the driveway etiquette for years with whomever moved in and trying to judge the quality of their potential neighbors by spying on all these strangers was foolish, Carolyn knew. It would only ever be an issue when both homeowners were leaving or arriving at exactly the same time, and how often was that likely? They would manage, Carolyn decided, and she and Palmer were here first. There were neighborhood expectations. She realized it was a small thing to be preoccupied with, and blamed the protectiveness on pregnancy.

Carolyn mentioned her surveillance only once to Palmer, one night at dinner, before their lives were upended, but downplayed the frequency and intensity of her habit.

"There's been a lot of interest in Frances's house," she said. "But have you noticed; nobody has kids?"

"I haven't," Palmer said. "Maybe they just don't bring their kids with them or since the house needs some work, people who don't have kids yet are mostly the ones looking."

Carolyn never had the chance to spy on the couple that bought the house, and their baby, when they toured the house with their agent. The July afternoon Julia and Jack Dailey made an offer on Frances's house, when Carolyn was twenty-four weeks pregnant, she and Palmer were at the movies, and she went into labor. By the time she came home from the hospital for good, after a week and two days of hoping for a miracle that didn't materialize, she'd forgotten about the rest of the world, and no longer cared about the house next door.

Palmer's family lived in town, and Graham, Ceci, and Anne flew out for the twins' funeral. And although they had neighbors and friends and work colleagues who brought food and sent cards and offered help, Carolyn couldn't wait for everyone to leave so that she could hide in private. Her grief was a barrier that shut everyone out.

In the early weeks after the girls died, the worst part of the day was the morning. When Carolyn first awoke, the refreshed reality was like driving a car whose brakes had failed head-on into a concrete wall. Every morning, she lived through the same fatal crash. Lying safely in bed offered no solace, so she got moving minutes after waking. Up and out of the bed. Feet on the floor. Out of pajamas and into clothes. Pants, bra, an actual shirt. Downstairs to pour a cup of coffee that the coffeemaker had been timed to brew the night before.

She would take her coffee to the backyard and drink it and mentally hasten the minutes by. She would shower later; she would make the bed later. She might or might not eat something that would qualify as breakfast before she had lunch. She might not eat either. The important thing was to go through as many motions and little daily ceremonies to get as far away as possible from waking up first thing in the morning and having the reality hit. One day she went in to get her second cup of coffee, and her throat tightened when she realized that with all this artificial hastening she was only getting herself closer to having to do the same thing again the next morning.

While the weeks of the summer passed and she remained secluded, instead of moving vans, contractors' trucks arrived every morning at Frances's house and continued to into the fall. Palmer told Carolyn the kitchen and bathrooms were being remodeled before the new owners moved in.

"He's a doctor," Palmer said. "That's what the guys working over there told me. He and his wife have a baby. A little boy."

In October they moved in—Julia, Jack, and their son Henry. Palmer and Carolyn waited a few days before they went over to introduce themselves. Because you never know if people drink or don't, or what they eat or don't eat, instead of a bottle of wine or lasagna, they took a jade plant. Everyone can use luck, she thought.

Carolyn still hadn't gone back to work, and she and Palmer were having a very hard time, but she told herself, *It's what you do*, and Carolyn stayed only as long as she felt like she could and not a minute longer, claiming she was fighting a cold, which also explained why she didn't shake either of their hands and kept her distance from their child. It was a terrible time for her to be meeting anyone new. Especially someone with a baby. Especially around the time her own baby girls were due.

After that day, they'd raise a hand when they saw each other coming and going, although Carolyn was hardly ever going anywhere, and because the wet fall Portland weather sent everyone indoors for a period of seclusion like it did every year, there was nothing peculiar about their lack of interaction. Perhaps after that first meeting Julia and Jack concluded that Carolyn and Palmer were aloof or shy or particular people, but Carolyn had enough trouble getting through every day that she didn't care. The one thing she did notice, and she found it funny in a profoundly sad way, considering how concerned she'd been at the beginning of the summer, was that sharing the driveway never posed a problem or caused any conflict. Julia's and Jack's schedules, and really, during that time only Palmer's, were such that there was virtually no overlap between their leaving their houses. It was just another factor that contributed to Palmer and Carolyn's remaining isolated in their grief, preventing them from reaching out in the way they would have otherwise.

As a therapist, Carolyn was well aware of the phenomenon that under certain circumstances it's easier to talk to strangers than the people closest to us, and she wasn't immune to it. That was precisely what led to the start of her friendship with Julia—Carolyn's unloading to her—the same December day that she and Palmer went to visit the girls' grave for the first time since the twins had died.

The day was frigid and clear, and they both cried at the cemetery, but they didn't talk. It was the first time they'd seen the single black granite marker they ordered adorned only with the girls' names in bronze, mounted in the order they were born:

GRACE

ABIGAIL

Although they had argued on the drive there, they were silent on the way home until Palmer pulled up in front of the house and told Carolyn he was going to his parents' for a few hours. He didn't invite her to join him, and she didn't ask to go. After she got out of the car, standing on the sidewalk and watching him drive away, Carolyn felt the familiar wave of panic grip and begin to build—*I'm alone, I'm alone, I'm alone. Help. I need help.* Almost six months after losing the girls it could still strike as acutely as it had the first time.

She had a bottle of Xanax in the house, but she didn't feel capable of going inside to get it. The only thing she felt capable of—as she often did when she was overcome by a panic attack—was walking. Carolyn knew what was happening in her brain and she knew how to breathe through it, but the distress was tenacious, like laughing in church. Once you're aware you're doing it and know you should stop, must stop, the one thing you absolutely cannot do is stop.

Carolyn did a lap around her block, counting backward from five hundred as she walked to the first corner, turned right, walked to the next corner, turned right, another block and still counting, two more right turns and then she was back on her street, passing Julia and Jack's house before walking past hers and starting a second lap. As she approached the middle of the block, Carolyn scanned the Daileys' windows for any activity inside. At some point, as eventually always happened, her mindful breathing pushed the panic away and the need to keep counting ceased. And although Carolyn didn't feel as intensely like she was coming undone as she had ten minutes earlier, she still had no desire to be in her house alone.

The next two times she passed Julia's house she thought she saw the movement of a person behind a curtain in an upstairs front window where a light was on. As it got darker and colder and she approached her house again, the thought of doing more laps was both a deterrent and an invitation; the colder it was, the more punishing it would be. She was wearing a hat and gloves and a down coat so she would keep walking, Carolyn decided, maybe until Palmer's car was back in front of their house. Maybe even after it had been there for a while.

This time when she was right in front of Julia's house, Carolyn saw her sitting on her front porch, also wearing a hat and gloves, and a down coat.

"Hi, Carolyn, right?" she said. "Do you want some company?"

Before Carolyn could answer Julia stood up and walked toward her. "I saw you out here and it reminded me how much I could use a walk."

And so they started the next lap together. Carolyn barely stopped before Julia joined her, and they were off again. As they walked, more lights came on inside people's living rooms and kitchens, and the occasional porch light.

They were quiet for the first few minutes then Julia said, "Is everything okay?"

"No. It's not." Carolyn started to cry. Not like she had sobbed earlier that afternoon, but that quickly her eyes were full. "Palmer and I went to the cemetery today. Where our twin daughters are buried. They were born in July. Premature. Right around the time you bought the house. Today was the first time we've been to visit. It's been more than five months."

She didn't know if Julia knew before Carolyn said anything, if Palmer had told her or Jack, or if she heard it from another neighbor. Julia had never seen Carolyn pregnant. It didn't matter. What mattered was that she said, "Oh, my God. I'm so very sorry, Carolyn. You've been living in hell all this time." What mattered was that she put her arm around Carolyn. What mattered was when Carolyn started to sob, Julia let her. What mattered was when they got to the next corner, and the next and the one after that—the same corners over and over again—they turned and kept walking. They kept walking past both their houses too many times to count. They kept walking after Palmer's car was back in front of Carolyn's house and her porch light and living room and kitchen lights were on. They kept walking after Palmer texted: *Where RU?* And Carolyn wrote back: *Walking with Julia. I'm OK.*

They kept walking while Julia listened, and Carolyn told her that she'd kissed another man the previous week when she was drunk at a work event she'd gone to with Palmer, and she was afraid her marriage was over. They kept walking while Julia told her when Jack was a resident, she had a miscarriage and the fact that Jack was a doctor offered her no comfort even though he had refused to leave her alone for days afterward.

They kept walking while Julia told her that her older brother died the night of his high school graduation when she was a sophomore and during the months that followed, she thought her parents' marriage was over. They kept walking while Carolyn told Julia her mother had died when she was nineteen and how some days, she still desperately needed her as much as she had as a feverish child.

By the time they stopped, they had both cried. Jack texted Julia twice, once to find out where she was, and once to let her know he had things under control with Henry and to stay out as long as she needed to. By the time they stopped, Palmer had texted Carolyn a second time to ask that she please, please come home.

By the time they stopped walking and finished talking that night, neither of them was the same person they'd been earlier that afternoon when Carolyn had circled their block all those times alone, and when Julia sat on her porch waiting, before she joined her.

2002

12

It was February and Graham's connecting flight out of O'Hare to New York was delayed until further notice, so he ordered another bourbon from the bartender. There was no reason to think he shouldn't get comfortable.

He was flying home after visiting Carolyn and Palmer in Portland for Carolyn's birthday. They'd been struggling after losing the twins the previous summer. That was the last time he'd been there. He flew out as soon as the girls were born and stayed until after the end. There's no right way to have a funeral for two babies who come too early, but one must be had. Graham's being there felt more futile than anything—wanting to help when there was nothing he or anyone else could do about the unbearable sadness and his daughter's private pain. When Carolyn needed her mother but only had him.

The bartender brought his drink and asked if he wanted him to change the channel. CNN was on with the sound off, the news ticker streaming along the bottom of the screens. Graham thanked him but said no, leave it.

A man walked in from the concourse, pulled out the stool two away from Graham's and sat down.

"Jesus Christ," he said.

The bartender put a square napkin in front of him. "You're back," he said.

"False alarm," the man said. "Bottle of Heineken. Thanks."

"You're stuck, too?" Graham asked.

"I am. Again, or still, I suppose," he said. "My ass and this stool have already spent four hours together today, and I thought I was finally getting out of here, but I get to the gate only to find out we're still delayed. The way this weather is, I don't know why I expected anything different. I'm settling in for the duration. And so should you." He looked at Graham's mostly full glass and raised his hand for the bartender and pointed.

"When you get a chance, another for him," the man said.

He asked where Graham was headed and where he'd come from and Graham told him, New York, and Portland.

"My wife and I are in New Canaan. I just flew out of JFK. Supposed to make a meeting in San Francisco if I ever get out of here. My daughter lives in Portland. She and her husband and my grandson," the man said. "Great city."

"Mine does, too," Graham said. "I was visiting her and my son-in-law. They've been having a hard time." He sipped his drink. "I forgot how tricky marriage can be. You don't get to rehearse so you know what to do when life beats you up a little."

The man looked down at his bottle. "Wouldn't that be nice," he said. "A marriage rehearsal." He stood up and moved over one to sit down on the stool next to Graham. "What's happening with them? If you don't mind my asking. Funny to have children who aren't anymore, isn't it?"

So Graham told him about Carolyn losing the girls, and that it had made her push her husband away, that she had just gone back to work in January, that she had kissed another man before Christmas, that she was afraid to try to get pregnant again.

"Poor kids," the man said. "So how was your visit then? Sounds like they're really up against it."

"I think they'll be all right," Graham said. "Maybe I'm just projecting but they're good together, they really are. I'd like her husband anyway, even if they weren't married. We'd be friends. He's in advertising, a very creative and interesting guy. I'd be his old friend and he would be my young one."

The man laughed. The bartender kept the drinks coming. The longer they talked, the more the conversation started to feel like their sole reason for being here—like they'd said, *If you're not busy tonight meet me at a bar at the airport*, instead of being there because they were both trapped.

"Someone's got to be hopeful," said the man. "Your being optimistic, that's got to mean something. Using your paternal powers of persuasion."

Graham realized that if they called his plane to board, he would have been disappointed.

"So you're married then, too?" the man asked.

"I was," Graham said. "I lost my wife, it's almost thirteen years now. Cancer."

"Jesus, I'm sorry," he said. "I thought you were an old married guy like me."

"I should be," said Graham.

"Yes," he said. "Yes, you should."

They sat there watching CNN. The bar had filled up since Graham arrived. People came and replaced people who left, until people kept coming but no one left and there was just standing room only. No one was going anywhere any time soon.

"You and your wife ever have that trouble?" the man said.

"No," Graham said. "We had three healthy girls. My youngest, that's who I was visiting."

"No," he said. "Marriage trouble. Someone's head getting turned."

Graham leaned on the bar. "Nothing I ever acted on. Wasn't worth it. And I'm a terrible liar. Once, a long time ago I was worried about my wife. But the truth is, I didn't want to know, and I didn't want to lose her. And honestly, I wasn't being a great husband. Like I said, there's no rehearsal." He felt like he was talking to an old friend he hadn't seen in a long time. Graham realized he'd never shared his fears about Joan with anyone. "What about you? Any rough water or all smooth sailing?"

"My wife and I have been through some very dark times. The very worst," the man said. "Our son died when he was seventeen. In a car accident. Before that I used to worry about death a lot, about going to hell, but I don't anymore. I've already been."

"My God," Graham said. "I don't know what to say. I'm so very sorry."

"It was a long time ago," he said. "But it's always with me. It's a terrible thing to have to get used to. My God, I can't remember the last time I told someone about him," He pushed the fingertips of his left hand against his forehead. "Christ, I'm sloppy."

"But you got through it?" Graham said. "You and your wife stayed together? People don't always when they lose a child. That's what I'm worried about."

"We did," he said. "I was afraid we wouldn't, but we did. Like someone said once, I can't remember who, we both never wanted to get divorced on the same day."

They seemed to be out of things to say then, like they had tied one another in some kind of painful morbid contest.

"You know I've got to call my wife and update her," the man said. "Plus I should walk and get a little air. I'm cutting myself off."

"I am, too," said Graham. "I'm afraid I've overdone it."

They stood and shook hands.

"Thanks for passing the time with me," Graham said. "Safe trip when you get on your way. Best of luck." It seemed wrong to say out loud that he had enjoyed talking with him, considering that between them they'd covered so much sad ground.

"I hope things work out for your daughter and her husband," the man said. "That they'll stay together and get back on track. That they can put their loss behind them. It won't ever disappear completely, but it'll get smaller in their rearview mirror. Trust me. Even if they split, they'll always have those babies between them."

Graham nodded to acknowledge his wise, painful words. "If I have an opportunity to share that with them, I will. I'm grateful for you saying that."

"People helping people," the man said. "Take care." He turned and walked straighter and faster than Graham guessed he was able, out of the bar toward the concourse, his briefcase in his left hand and his coat draped over the bend of his right elbow.

It wasn't until he was watching his retreating back that Graham realized they hadn't introduced themselves. During their intense discussion the man volunteered intimate details about his life and family, as had Graham, but they'd never exchanged names.

PORTLAND

2014

13

This is the twenty-third trip Graham has made to Portland since Carolyn moved to the West Coast in 1994 for graduate school and stayed. And although Joan has been gone twenty-five years, every time he flies across the country he is still incredulous it's been that long. Waiting in line at security with his shoes off, when the flight attendants pass by with their carts offering snacks or meals, coffee, soda, wine or cocktails, when he's returning from the restroom scanning for the identifying back of a stranger's head to return to his seat, looking at the rows' numbers as he gets closer, when he's pulling his bag from the overhead bin after they've landed. All those insignificant moments remind him it still feels unnatural that he's traveling alone.

This is a trip Joan has never made. But when they're taxiing to take off, that's when Graham closes his eyes—every time he flies anywhere—and imagines Joan next to him, holding her hand in his and telling her: *Here we go, darling.*

Graham has a journal where he's listed the trips he's made to Portland with corresponding dates and notes detailing what happened while he was there. He'll do the same thing for this trip. It's all relatively unimportant, but fun to look back on. The local attractions, restaurants, venues where they saw a play or show, trips to the coast or the mountains. The reason for the trip if there was one: when he met Palmer in

1996; their wedding two years later; in 2001 for the twins. That was a terrible goddamn year.

He's not sure why but he doesn't keep journals for his visits with Ceci and Anne. Maybe it's because Carolyn is the baby. Her sisters' feelings might be hurt if they knew he didn't document his time with them the same way. When he visits the two of them and their families Graham always takes pictures, though, too many. One way or another he tries not to miss anything.

It's Monday of Thanksgiving week so the airport is crowded, and the plane is full, although that's always true no matter when he flies anymore, no matter what time of year. He'll stay through the holiday and weekend and head home a week from today. Graham loves being in the middle of their lives when he visits, but he does wish where Carolyn had found happiness and made her home wasn't so far away. The distance between them makes Graham feel obsolete.

He's only half kidding when he teases her that if she lived closer, he would feel younger. She reminds him if *he* moved closer to her—traded in the Big Apple for Douglas firs and cleaner air—he'd add years to his life, turn back the clock a bit, which he wouldn't mind doing. It's disorienting to be as old as he is. On paper Graham knows it's true, but seventy-four is for his old, frail, arthritic grandmother who died when he was twelve. He runs two miles three times a week and plays golf at least two. *To hell with you, seventy-four,* he thinks. *Believe me, I don't look my age.* And despite his resistance, Anne—his middle girl—finally wore him down with her insistence that he's always been cutting edge and now isn't the time to stop, and convinced Graham to make a Facebook page.

So now he's on Facebook, and under his profile picture next to the silhouette icon for friends is the number eight. His friend list is comprised of his three daughters, two of his sons-in-law, and his three oldest grandchildren. It's funny, when he talks to the men at the club about how his family's doing he tells them, *Yes, the girls and I are Facebook friends.* Some of them are online friends with their kids, too, and once one of them brings it up, they all pick up their phones and scroll through the pictures of their grandchildren.

While he thinks it's a poor replacement for phone calls and the photographs the girls used to send in the mail, Graham appreciates some things about the technology. The messages and photos they text, and he can see seconds later, sent from hundreds or thousands of miles away. And they all Skype, it's the next best thing to being there, but he is disappointed there's not much worthwhile that comes in the mail anymore. Every month it's a bunch of junk mixed in with the few bills Graham still has. And then there are the things he didn't see coming and didn't have time to prepare for.

Cecelia, his oldest, was the one who put the quip on her Facebook page poking fun at herself when she turned fifty: *Inside every older person is a young person wondering what the hell happened.* Joan never saw forty-nine and being reminded in that particular way that Ceci was older than her mother ever was kept him off Facebook for several days. It wasn't her fault Graham was struck the way he was. The post was a jarring reminder he hadn't expected, like a billboard advertising a missing child that millions of people never notice, but you find unsettling because she went to your daughter's school.

Twenty-five years is a long time to have been alone, there's no question about it, and looking back, wasn't something Graham planned. After a point he tried to be as open as he could be for finding another, if not a wife, then a partner; if not another love, then someone he liked very much and in whose company he was happier than he was alone. Given how beloved Joan had been, and how social they had been as a couple, there was no shortage of well-meaning friends who thought highly of available women they knew, friends of friends, ladies they wanted him to meet—*What do you say, Graham? It's just a few hours for one night. But certainly you don't have to.*

So over the years there have been a lot of dinners, nights at the theater, brunches and visits to museums and galleries. Sometimes the two of them have ended up in bed, and because he tried not to lead anyone on, hopefully there were no broken hearts. But that's been the extent of it. Graham was willing to be surprised if he found a woman with that unidentifiable something, one who would seem like a natural, permanent or long-term fixture, but it just never happened. So he became a confirmed widower. It hasn't bothered him, and he hasn't been unhappy. He knows the girls have wondered and worried, but he thinks they finally get it.

Graham is typically not a brooder, but air travel always makes him wistful. There are only a handful of things to do when you're flying across the country. Since he's on his way to see Carolyn, he thinks about her. He's always associated her, more than Cecilia and Anne, with that time of Joan's illness and death. Even now that she's been married to Palmer for sixteen years and is raising two boys, everyone healthy and well, to Graham, Carolyn is still the college kid who took a break from school to be home with him and Joan from the start of when things got bad and stayed until the end.

And after it was over, Graham practically had to kick her out to get her to return to school the next fall. The truth was he hadn't known what he would have done without Carolyn, and if he hadn't made her leave when he did, as much as he feared being by himself, he was afraid he would have turned into a pathetic, lonely man who trapped his daughter into staying and caring for him. He had refused to do that to her.

He knows Joan would love Portland's west coast friendliness and quirky reputation. Graham can imagine her finding them a granny condo so they could visit more frequently and regularly. He knows what she'd say: *Graham, I made an appointment with a real estate agent. I said we only want to look.*

But since it's only Graham, a condo isn't necessary. Carolyn knows so many people, just like her, who grew up on the East Coast and then left it for the Northwest. And now, she tells her father, their parents, many, but not all, now retired, have moved west too to be near their children and grandchildren, or they've bought the granny condo, making it that much easier to visit whenever they want.

It's all part of my campaign to get you out of New York, Dad, she has told him.

Just this past year, her neighbor Julia's parents moved to Portland from New Canaan.

"You'll meet them when you're here," she told Graham during their last phone call. "Hutch and Alice. They're great. It's going to be a great week, Dad."

But Carolyn knows Graham can't choose her and Portland over Ceci and her family in Boston, or Anne and her family in Chicago. And he can't give up the apartment that he and Joan moved into when they were first married. It's his home and it's the girls' home, with enough room for everyone to visit at the same time, even if it's a bit crowded. He's never wanted them to have to decide whose turn it is to spend a holiday with him. When his girls want to come home, they can all come at once.

The week ahead is supposed to be dry with some days of sun— "I ordered good Portland weather for you, Dad," Carolyn told him—and Thanksgiving has always been Graham's favorite holiday. Plus, they'll get a chance for a good long visit. He will grill his special steaks one night, play some golf with Palmer, and insist the two of them go out for a night by themselves while he watches his grandsons.

The other thing he'll do is delicate, but important. Graham will bring it up because he knows Carolyn won't. It's a kind of script they never deviate from. Tomorrow morning, maybe during his second cup of coffee, he'll ask, *When will we go see the girls?*

And although he'll have been the one to mention it, Carolyn will have already decided and will tell him the time and day when they'll drive to the cemetery where Grace and Abigail are buried. Graham feels the same way about Carolyn's babies' grave as he does Carolyn: he wishes it weren't so far away. Just like he does back home with their grandmother's grave, he'd like to be able to visit it as much as he wants, any time he wants.

14

With so much construction in the city, it's impossible to gauge traffic so Carolyn is at the airport to pick up her father far earlier than she planned.

She feels too young to be forty-four. Since each of them turned forty, every year when she and Ceci and Anne creep a number closer to forty-eight, it's the first thing they talk about on the phone during the birthday call, usually after a glass of wine or two. Ceci is already fifty-one, Anne, forty-nine. Everyone is healthy, they each have a mammogram every year, they check themselves, but they've all been afraid. People survive their forties every day, but their mother didn't. They have all tested negative for the gene mutation, so their discussions typically end after one of them says, *It's just a number.*

But Carolyn knows what powerful significance numbers can have to people, what grim or hopeful indicators they are. As a therapist, she strives to help her clients overcome or accept or eliminate trouble from their lives, and numbers are part of it more often than you'd think.

I've been divorced for five years. I thought I'd be remarried by now.

I haven't had a drink in thirteen months.

He's been dead now for twelve years and some days it feels like it just happened.

We've only been married for eight months and already we're having problems.

They mean different things to different people. Ways to get through the day, signs of success or failure, marks of progress or first steps taken.

Carolyn has her own important numbers. At twenty-four weeks, her twin girls were born. Seven days is how long she and Palmer had Grace, and nine days and four and a half hours is how long they had her sister Abigail. Five is the number of months she and Palmer didn't have sex after they died. One is the number of times during those five months that she kissed another man. Zero is the number of times they visited the twins' grave in those five months. One is the number of infant caskets they buried them in together. The girls would be thirteen now, middle schoolers, preparing for their freshman year. She thinks: *You can always rely on the solidity of numbers, whether you like their truths or not.*

She really is early. Graham's flight is on time and Carolyn still has at least twenty minutes to kill. She gets a coffee at Starbucks and takes a photo of her shoes against the iconic airport carpet that will soon be replaced. The upcoming remodel inspires countless travelers to take their own shoe-and-carpet photos as a drawn-out farewell homage to the trademark pattern. Carolyn can imagine Joan asking, *Why is this a thing? Airport carpet?*

Because it's Portland, Mom. People say "Keep Portland Weird" for a reason.

She posts the picture on her Facebook page with the hashtag #pdxcarpet and the comment, *Picking up Grandpa!* She tags her father so that "Graham Cavanaugh" is highlighted in blue, then adds #lifeisgood!

Over the years, one of the ways Carolyn has coped with missing her mother is to imagine, in a variety of situations, really ponder, what Joan would have done. Palmer was the one who co-opted the evangelicals' acronym WWJD and made it their own: *What Would Joan Do?*

Now the whole family uses it.

The first time she deeply considered the idea was a little over a year after the girls died, when she and Palmer started to talk about getting pregnant again. Carolyn had become so undone after losing them, she almost lost her marriage, too, and she knows that a lesser man than Palmer might have walked away. The thought of being pregnant again terrified her no matter how much confidence the doctors shared about their successfully rolling the dice again. That was the only way Carolyn could think about pregnancy, as a risky, unwise gamble, a looming minefield.

Since she couldn't talk to her, Carolyn was left imagining what Joan would have done or said to help her decide about trying again. Part of the reason WWJD was both useful and a comfort was because when she was alive, her mother had naturally been a source of sound—while not always desirable—advice.

During her three-year battle with breast cancer, Joan remained—or at least she appeared to everyone—unshaken by what she was up against. She wasn't in denial, but she planned—she expected—to prevail, and swinging at that. She didn't see surviving meekly as an option. Joan's determination was what was most evident during her last six months. She resented being the reason for Carolyn interrupting her education, and they had fought about it bitterly when Carolyn told her she wasn't returning to school after Christmas break her freshman year.

Because Joan was proud, she would have been angry no matter what, but what had been Carolyn's misstep, what had fueled Joan's anger and could have been avoided, was

Carolyn's decision not to return to Amherst for the second semester without telling her mother. Carolyn had told her father—she didn't ask his permission—and Graham spoke to the dean, but neither of them said anything about it to Joan until Carolyn didn't start packing when she should have. Carolyn couldn't blame her mother for feeling deceived and demeaned. She and Graham should have handled it differently, but they were all in uncharted territory. If there was a right way to do things, it was not obvious to any of them, and it was easy to make a mistake.

Before Carolyn decided to stay home, she promised herself that until Joan was well again, she wouldn't fight with her. She wanted the time they spent together to be without strife—being nineteen, Carolyn mistakenly thought she had control over such a thing. She didn't. There was still strife. They had it the first week in January.

Carolyn couldn't remember the last time she'd seen her mother so enraged. Joan rarely gave herself over to that degree of anger, so the occasions when it happened were isolated and memorable. The intensity of her emotion was evident in how quietly she spoke; her restraint was more threatening than if she'd been shrieking loudly enough to alarm the neighbors.

"How dare you leave school without discussing it with me first? I'm your mother and I'm still very much alive. You can't wait until I'm dead to do something I disapprove of? You'll have plenty of time then, believe me."

After she finished talking, Carolyn had to look away to avoid her wounded stare.

There was nothing Joan could do or say that would make Carolyn spoil for a fight. She'd already decided she would wait her out. Joan made that almost impossible.

Carolyn said she was doing it for Graham's sake, that he was the one who needed her, not Joan.

"It's not always about you, Mom," Carolyn said. "Just because you're sick doesn't mean everything is about you."

It was a criticism no one would ever utter to someone whose days were numbered, but because her mother's days had not seemed numbered, what Carolyn said didn't seem out of line. She was sure—everyone was—the cancer wasn't going to kill Joan. They had all been blindly confident.

So Carolyn consistently refused to engage when Joan baited her and rode out the times when the gloves came off and Joan got ugly, got ugly out of her system, apologized and they continued as before, until the next time. Joan faced her disease head on, and since she was battling something she couldn't see, if fighting vicariously with whoever was closest at hand helped bolster her determination and resilience, Carolyn obliged by being a willing, thick-skinned surrogate.

Even on her bad days punctuated by bouts of sickness, Joan refused to yield the upper hand. One late morning after she had been violently ill, she walked out of the bathroom and closed the door behind her, stood in the hallway with her forehead and clenched right hand pressed against the wall, her legs trembling and whispered through gritted teeth—as quietly and angrily as she'd spoken to Carolyn when she realized she wasn't returning to college—"Fuck you, fuck you, fuck you."

Joan reserved profanity for the times when she thought it was called for, and although she didn't hold back when those occasions arose, her selectivity prevented her from ever seeming vulgar.

Carolyn was in second grade when Joan sat the three of them down and went through a comprehensive glossary of expletives and their definitions. Anne, who was a seventh grader, had muttered *fuck* while she was doing math homework and their mother saw it as a teachable moment. Ceci,

Anne, and Carolyn sat there with their mouths gaping while she spoke.

Everyone knows all the words. Your father does, I do, your teachers do, your friends' parents know too. Everyone. The older you get the more you're going to hear them, so let's get the mystery out of the way. Swearing seems interesting only because you're told not to do it. I'd prefer you didn't swear—cursing children just look like tiny tyrants with lousy parents and terrible manners—but if you must try it, please do it at home. Kids don't realize, if you swear every time you open your mouth, it becomes meaningless; it's like not swearing at all. Save it for when you want to make a point. And because I want you to understand exactly what you're saying, here's what they all mean.

Each time she introduced an offensive word and its definition, one after another, she unfolded an accompanying finger from her fist. After she finished and was silent, her open palms and challenging expression invited her daughters' comments or questions if they had any. None of them did.

Carolyn didn't know if it was part of the plan or not, but hearing their mother utter that barrage of forbidden words in an unexpected, unorthodox tutorial served as a natural deterrent for swearing. She remembered for a long time afterward it simply no longer held any attraction for the three of them.

Almost a year after losing the girls, the following spring, Carolyn still feared another failed pregnancy, and privately wrestled with that worry all the time; it was her constant companion: stuck in traffic, pushing a cart through the grocery store, the few minutes between clients' appointments, showering, trying to fall asleep at night, upon waking first thing in the morning, making love with Palmer—always protected sex.

She told Julia how terrified she was, and when she finally could, Carolyn shared her anxieties with Palmer about trying again. She tried to combat her thoughts about their first tragic experience as short-lived parents by imagining what her mother would do or tell Carolyn to do. She knew Joan never would have let her fears keep her from fighting for what she wanted, even if she was afraid. Carolyn believed Joan would tell her and Palmer to try again. Palmer said he thought they should, but only if Carolyn felt ready, and she told him she was.

★ ★ ★

While she scans the arriving passengers leaving the terminal to where she's waiting for her father, out of the corner of her eye Carolyn sees a former client, Audrey, and another woman, walking together from a different concourse toward the escalators that lead to baggage claim.

Two years earlier, Audrey had started seeing Carolyn after her husband, Leo, a firefighter, died in a skiing accident on Mt. Hood, leaving Audrey to raise their three sons alone. They worked together for six months while Audrey processed her grief, and struggled with a blossoming relationship with her late husband's oldest friend. After working together for that amount of time, Audrey said she felt like she had a solid foundation of tools and coping skills to move forward on her own. Carolyn had liked Audrey; she was one of those rare clients whom Carolyn could see befriending if they'd met under other circumstances.

One of the stipulations in Carolyn's contract with her clients is that if they ever encounter each other in public, Carolyn defers to the clients to decide if they wish to initiate acknowledging each other, or not. It's an awkward necessity, and the occasions that demand its existence happened more than Carolyn ever would have thought. She's run into clients at the grocery store, at the Oregon Coast, and at yoga. Once, in a gentle vinyasa class that Carolyn didn't return to, a client, Rebecca, was two rows in front of her, for an hour going through the same poses as Carolyn. Neither before nor after the class did Rebecca indicate she recognized her and didn't mention it in their next session.

Rebecca's prerogative that day was the most uncomfortable scenario Carolyn's job as a therapist outside her office had put her in, but her choice didn't bother Carolyn. She'd sincerely thought, *Good for her*. Rebecca, an incest survivor, had long struggled with establishing and maintaining boundaries, so Carolyn was silently proud of her resolve.

But, for her own part, Carolyn wasn't interested in having her own vulnerability on display with a client in the same room while they both sweated and stretched, breathed from their cores and quieted their minds.

When she checks the airport monitor again, she sees that Graham's flight has arrived and her phone pings with alerts. Fifteen Facebook friends like her post and someone, not really a friend in real life, a former school parent who has since moved to Houston, who clearly hasn't read Carolyn's post carefully, has commented: *Ooh, are you going somewhere? Fun!* Another not true friend, another therapist in town, has liked the comment. Carolyn should do a thorough Facebook purge, really; people make it so obvious when it's time.

Then she hears her name and looks up and finally, there is her father, waving as he passes the people in front of him, striding toward Carolyn with his arms outstretched.

15

Alice and Hutch have lived in Portland for five months, since the beginning of the summer.

Although they had a countless string of dreadful nights after Mark died, one of which included a long meeting with a real estate agent whose daughter was a classmate of Julia's, in the sober light of day the idea of putting the house on the market seemed to exacerbate their loss rather than diminish it, so they managed to survive that raw time, and after almost forty years, finally sold the place to move across the country to be near Julia and her family. Ultimately, their desire to be closer to one child proved to be a more powerful motivator than their futile wish to flee their despair over the other.

It wasn't the only time they considered moving, leaving New York and the whole tri-state area behind for a new start somewhere else with no painful history. September 9th, 2001, was Hutch and Alice's thirty-fifth wedding anniversary, and they were spending a week on Nantucket when the attacks happened. Although they had flown to the island, they took the ferry back to the mainland and rented a car to drive home, cutting their trip short by two days. Morgan Stanley lost ten employees, only one of whom Hutch knew, and not well, but he and Alice attended all of the funerals.

The shock of having no office, and no building to return to, was its own bottomless grief. In the end, their temptation to leave was far weaker than their committed resolve to join and maintain the resilient solidarity that united New Yorkers, and the rest of the country, in the wake of the tragedy.

Hutch likes the Pacific Northwest and this city very much. The City of Roses, what a lovely thing to be known for. He's always liked it, since Julia decided to call it home, and he likes even more about it now that it's home for him and Alice too. But it is much smaller than New York, which was the axis of his life for so many years, and perhaps that's why he's always tacking on the diminutive attribution—their little place, their little balcony, their little neighborhood café—without intending to be critical or insulting.

They have a two-bedroom in Indigo Apartments, a LEED Platinum Certified building that impresses Hutch as much as any building in New York ever did. It's near the Pearl District, a downtown neighborhood which used to be the gritty warehouse part of the city but is now very tony and hip, *Just like your mother and me*, he's told Julia. There's room on their balcony for Alice's lavender, lobelia, and miniature roses, and Hutch and Alice drink their coffee there most mornings, even when it rains. The weather makes it that much better. Their grandsons come over and spend the night a few times a month, and in August, Julia and Jack joined them for several dinners on the rooftop patio.

When Hutch walks the waterfront loop alongside the Willamette, as he does three mornings a week, he thinks, *This is what retirement is, what a snapshot of being seventy-four years old looks like.* It still feels like a mystery to him how he ended up in an old man's body and has an adult child who has made babies of her own.

Hutch wasn't bored—there had been so much involved in their cross-country move, it tested his sanity—but after the flurry died down and they were settled, he didn't have very much to do. He ran the one idea he came up with by Alice one morning over coffee out on the balcony, knowing that if she could think of something better, she wouldn't hesitate to tell him.

"I've been thinking about taking a class," Hutch said. "You've got all kinds of things going on with Julia and the kids and starting to volunteer at the museum, but I've got too much time on my hands, so I thought I'd find a class to take. An art class. What do you think?"

"Wonderful idea," said Alice. "You were always so good, and you loved it."

So now he's enrolled in the drawing class at Portland Northwest College of Art on Thursday nights from six-thirty to nine-thirty.

After he registered, Hutch told Alice, "I found one I'm really excited about—a class." Then in the way of a defense that wasn't called for: "A little drawing class."

There was the diminutive attribution again, diminishing a thing that he felt no condescension toward. He felt the opposite—he was excited—and maybe that was what Hutch was trying to temper, his enthusiasm. He couldn't think of the last time he had done something that was his alone, aside from work, but even that was shared with colleagues.

It's obvious that Hutch is the oldest student in the class, but consistent with what he's discovered about the Northwest mindset, no one seems to care, or even notice. He still has his drawings of Joan, ten altogether, in a manila folder at the bottom of a box. Proof of Hutch's secret, decades old, but that he can't bear to part with. Even though they are worn and soft with age, you can still see the likeness—he has to admit, he was pretty good. Anyone who knew Joan at that age and saw the drawings couldn't mistake her for anyone else. He's never worried about them. The box dates back to his time at

NYU and contains the rest of his portfolio from that year. He has moved the box from his parents' place, to Philadelphia, to the two apartments and one house where he and Alice and their family lived, and now, finally, to the closet at The Indigo where they keep their suitcases and vacuum cleaner.

★ ★ ★

He hasn't looked at the drawings in years. He did after Mark died, when as much as Hutch tried to resist the flood of arrogance, he worried that Mark's death was punishment for his relationship with Joan, even though he didn't believe God worked that way and would never have taken his son and broken his wife's heart because of something Hutch had done when he was twenty-three. He had wanted someone to blame for Mark's death and had felt like he deserved to assume guilt. And it had been a way to attempt to tamp his grief by distracting himself from it with an unrelated regret. His thoughts often circled to that place, until one day they didn't anymore.

But right after he ended it with Joan, after Hutch moved to Philadelphia, he looked at the drawings whenever he was compelled, which initially was often—out of heartbreak and loneliness and indulgence in the proof that he'd had Joan in his life at all. In lieu of photographs of the two of them that didn't exist, or letters or gifts they'd never exchanged, they were the only evidence—and flimsy at best—of what they'd shared; they were *drawings*, for God's sake, he would think when he was feeling sorry for himself. They weren't the unequivocal example of the affair. When mere weeks after arriving in Philadelphia, he met Alice at the Broad Street Diner, when they each took one of the last two seats at the counter, the surprise of being newly smitten buoyed him out of his self-pity.

Over time, because of his dedication as a husband, father and breadwinner, Hutch stopped looking at the drawings. It was a comfort to know where they were, but the embarrassment of riches in his life had replaced the need to visit the memories the drawings invoked, until they lost Mark.

The only other time Hutch remembers so clearly looking at them was after he learned about Joan's death, twenty-five years ago. Four years after Mark.

As soon as he'd been able, in the house alone, Hutch pulled out all ten drawings from the bottom of the box in the attic, laid them out on the dusty floor and wept again. He had wept earlier in the men's room at his office in the World Trade Center after he got the letter, which had been mailed to him at work. He didn't recognize the handwriting or the return address in Charlottesville, Virginia.

He still has the letter. It's in the box with the drawings of Joan.

September 23, 1989

Dear Mr. Hutchinson,

We don't know each other but I was a family friend of Joan Cavanaugh's. I'm very sorry to be the bearer of sad news, especially in this form, a letter from a stranger. After bravely fighting breast cancer for three years, she lost the fight six months ago in March. But before her death Joan told me of her friendship with you and asked me if, after she passed away, I would notify you. Because of my own sadness and then discomfort, I've delayed in doing so and for that I apologize, too. Again, I heartily apologize for sharing this news so abruptly, but because it was something Joan asked of me, I knew it was important and honoring her request was the least I could do.

Sincerely yours,

Peter Herring

It was a shock, for so many reasons. So soon after Mark. That Joan had told someone, this family friend, also named Peter, about them, about him. That back then, with no internet or Google, this Peter Herring had found him. That she was only forty-eight. And the letter begged more questions than it answered: Had she still been married to Graham? Did she have any more children after Ceci? What kind of friend was this man and how had he known her? Hutch was tempted to call information, get the number of this Peter Herring and pick up the phone. He imagined all sorts of outcomes. Hutch could ask this fellow every question he had until Peter Herring told him everything he wanted to know.

But this frivolous idea also invited its unwelcome companion, shame. The idea of engaging in such unproductive, clandestine behavior made Hutch feel exactly as he had when he'd slunk around Joan's apartment building decades earlier, biding his time for any glimpse of her from afar. There was nothing to be gained from questioning Herring and, Hutch knew in all honesty—he was too old not to—that the only thing he could expect from any of the wild pursuits he entertained was a deeper, emptier feeling of futility. Nothing alleviated losing Joan back then—only time, and Alice—and after so many years there was nothing to soften the truth of her death.

But a week after he'd gotten the letter, a week during which Alice asked Hutch multiple times every day if he was all right, he dropped a postcard in the mail to the address in Virginia.

Dear Peter Herring,

Thank you for writing to me. It was not an easy task Joan asked of you and I wanted to let you know your letter arrived and how much I appreciate you sending it.

Yours truly,

Peter Hutchinson

Writing back, even that brief note, felt like a small measure of control Hutch could exercise and contribute to closure. He and Joan would never cross paths again, not in this lifetime, and as final as the fact of that matter was, he came to think of the news of her death as a blessing. He was grateful for the odd fortune of getting such a letter, unexpected as it was, because for as little as it told him, it was enough to know that Joan would never grow into an old, diminished woman, and that Hutch could stop wondering if he would ever see her again.

★ ★ ★

Alice and Hutch are at Julia and Jack's for dinner, and Hutch and Julia are making pad thai. Cooking together is their thing. Alice, Jack, and their neighbors Carolyn and Palmer are in the living room drinking wine and visiting and one of their sons is watching TV with Julia's boys. Carolyn's father is coming for Thanksgiving in a few weeks and at some point, he and Alice will meet him, Julia tells Hutch. She and Carolyn are full of plans.

"Shit," Julia says. "I swore we had soy sauce but we're out. Dad, can you go next door and check Carolyn's, so no one has to run to the store? It's the cabinet to the left of the stove, bottom shelf. The back door's open."

Hutch walks out of Julia's yard, crosses the driveway, opens the gate to Carolyn and Palmer's yard, shuts it behind him and walks into the house. Inside the back door is a mudroom and through that, the kitchen, connected to a family room off to the side. He finds the soy sauce where Julia said it would be, but instead of leaving, Hutch walks into the dining room.

The dining room table is covered with a sewing project: a state-of-the-art machine, folded yards of fabric, cut quilt blocks—some in stacked piles, some already sewn together. From the look of the patterns, pastel blue Winnie-the-Pooh, and white polka dots on a yellow background, Hutch guesses Carolyn is working on a baby quilt.

By now he's almost in the living room. He walks toward the mantel to look at the photographs lined up there. In an ornate silver frame is a photo of Carolyn and Palmer on their wedding day and several pictures of their two sons at various ages in different sized frames. Hutch passes the fireplace to get a better look at the photos at the far end of the mantel.

When Hutch sees the photograph of Joan on her wedding day, he has to reach out and steady himself on the arm of the chair behind him. It's the same picture he had seen in her and Graham's apartment fifty years earlier.

He stands staring at the photo, hanging onto the chair, then he lets go of the chair and walks to the mantel. He picks up the frame and sits down in the same chair which had just steadied him. He gazes at the face he'd known so well.

"Hello?" Hutch is startled by a voice behind him.

He turns around, the frame in his hands, and there's Carolyn's other son at the foot of the stairs.

"Oh, hello there," Hutch says. "I'm Julia's dad. I'm Hutch."

"I'm Brett," he says. He looks to be around ten or eleven.

"Well, hello, Brett, it's nice to meet you. I'm very sorry," Hutch says. What else can he say? He stands up and returns the picture to the mantel. "Julia sent me over here to get soy sauce—" he points to where he'd set it down on the dining room table, near the quilt project, as if it's to blame for his prowling.

"There it is, over there, and your folks have such a nice house I just started snooping around. I saw your mom's sewing, and then I just started looking at all these great pictures of your family."

"It's cool," Brett says. "I like to check out people's houses, too. One of my friend's houses has a bidet in one of their bathrooms. It was already there when they moved in. It's super weird."

Hutch doesn't plan to say any more than is necessary, but caught, he feels like he has to do something, so off he goes, before he can even stop himself.

"Who is this?" he points to the frame he'd just put back.

"My grandmother Joan," Brett says. "My mom's mom. She died when my mom was in college. We visit her grave when we go to New York. That's where my grandparents lived. My grandfather still does."

"Oh, I see," Hutch says. He stares at the frame. "I'm very sorry to hear that."

"How come you were holding it?"

He scrambles to answer the kid's question, which has taken longer than Hutch thought it would for him to ask.

"Well, like I said, I was admiring your family's photos. I was being nosy; I really am sorry. And when I saw this picture, it reminded me of someone I knew years ago. But after I had a closer look, I see it's not the person I was thinking of." Hutch laughs as he tries to make his words convincing. "Supposedly we all have a twin out there somewhere, right?"

He walks away from the mantel, and Brett, and toward the soy sauce on the dining room table, which seems much farther away than it is.

"I should head back next door," Hutch says. "Julia's in the middle of cooking."

"That would be pretty wild," Brett says. "If you'd known my grandmother."

Hutch retrieves the soy sauce and continues into the kitchen, making for the back door. *Just put one foot in front of the other*, he thinks. *Christ.*

Brett follows him and gets a glass from the cabinet next to the sink. Hutch stops when he gets to the back door and turns around. He wants to ask Brett to not rat him out, but that would call more attention to what he'd caught Hutch doing, so he goes with another tack.

"I'm sorry you never knew your grandmother," Hutch says. "I was good friends with my grandmother, and I like being a friend to my grandsons."

His playing at lightheartedness is taking more energy than Hutch expected. He feels like he needs to lie down and rest.

"Yeah," Brett says. "It's sad. We talk about her a lot though." He fills the glass with water from the tap. "So who was she?" he asks.

"What?" Hutch says.

"Who's the woman you thought the picture of my grandmother was? Was she your girlfriend?" Brett says.

The cordless landline on the counter rings and Brett peers at the caller ID. He thumbs toward Julia's house. "They probably wonder what happened to you," he says. He picks up the phone, presses a button and holds it to his ear. "Hello," and after a few seconds, "Yeah, he's here, he's on his way back now. Yeah, I'll be over in a minute. Okay, bye." He pushes another button and puts the phone back on the counter. "Like I said," Brett says.

Brett smiles at him and Hutch wonders if he recognizes, as Hutch does, the strangeness of the reversed roles they're in: He's the waylaid kid on an errand, his delay warranting checking on, and Brett is the trusted neighbor assuring Hutch's family he's heading home momentarily.

"So was she like a girlfriend?" he says.

The phone call from Julia's house hasn't rescued Hutch from answering. "No, not really," he says. "I had hoped so, but things didn't turn out that way."

"What was her name?" Brett says.

"Sorry, Brett, I have to get back," Hutch says. "What does it matter?"

"You could find her if you wanted to," Brett says. "You can find practically anyone on the internet."

Hutch draws a blank for a beat, thinks of his grandmother and makes her the substitute.

"Margot," he says. "Her name was Margot. That's who I thought your grandmother was. A woman I used to know named Margot."

"Well, if you ever want any help looking her up, let me know," Brett says. "I helped my grandfather find some friends he went to high school with. It really blew his mind."

"Okay, I'll remember that. Thanks, Brett," Hutch says. "I'll see you later." Because he can't think of anything else to say or do, he raises the bottle of soy sauce in the gesture of a toast, as if it's a meaningful prop.

"Sure, Hutch, see you later," he says.

As Hutch walks back to Julia's house he thinks about the irony of Brett's offer. He wasn't looking for Joan—he'd known for almost twenty-five years what happened to her—and yet he'd stumbled on her anyway, in the house right next to his daughter's.

There was no way he could continue the evening they all started less than an hour ago, but that now seemed like a different time. To finish cooking with Julia and be in the same room with and talk to Carolyn is just too much. Hutch delivers the soy sauce and kisses his daughter on the forehead and tells her he's so sorry but he's feeling chilled, maybe it's a fever coming on, and he's going to take a cab home. He barely glances at Carolyn and Palmer visiting with Alice, asks them to excuse his interruption, and tells Alice the same story, kisses her on the forehead, and announces he's leaving. She asks if he wants her to come with him and Hutch tells her no, he doesn't want to ruin her night, and Alice asks if he's sure and Hutch says that yes, he is, really, and that he'll see her at home.

16

At dinner on the second night of Graham's visit, his grandson Brett tells them a strange story. Carolyn is talking about when all the parents—her neighbor Julia's parents, and Graham—are going to meet. She and Julia are thinking of hosting brunch together the Sunday after Thanksgiving, before Graham goes back to New York, or maybe they'll just have drinks together one night, keep it simple and easy. Carolyn and Julia already have to work hard enough one day this week.

"Hey, Mom, you know Hutch, right?" Brett says. "He saw Grandma's picture and thought it was someone he knew."

"What?" says Carolyn. "What are you talking about? When?"

"Julia's dad knew Grandma?" Kyle says.

"No, Kyle, he was *wrong*," says Brett, condescending to his brother, who is eight, two years younger than Brett. "Like I said, he *thought* it was someone he knew, but it was a mistake."

"Hang on," Carolyn says. "When did this happen?"

"Ease up, Brett," Palmer says. "Bud, what are you talking about?"

"I don't know. It was after Halloween when he was at Julia's cooking dinner or something," Brett says. "She sent him over here to borrow something, and I came downstairs after I finished my homework, and I was about to walk over to Julia's for dinner and found him in the living room looking at that picture of Grandma."

"That seems a little weird," Palmer says. "What did you say to him?"

"I asked him what he was doing, and we talked a little bit and he finally said he thought she was someone named Margot," Brett says. "Geez, it's not a big deal. I just wanted to contribute to the conversation."

"Who did he say Margot was?" says Carolyn. "Sorry, one more question."

Brett sighs. "I don't know, dude. Someone he liked but wasn't his girlfriend. Ask him yourself. Since it wasn't Grandma what does it even matter?"

"*Dude?*" Carolyn says. "Really?"

"Sorry, Mom," he says.

After dinner, the boys are excused and Palmer starts to clear the table. "You two sit," he says to Carolyn and Graham.

"What did you make of that?" Graham says. "What Brett said. Is everything all right with Julia's father, like cognitively?"

"He's fine. I don't know, Dad," says Carolyn. "Maybe Mom has a doppelganger out there somewhere. Someone named Margot."

"Where did he grow up?" says Graham. "Julia's dad. Do you know?"

"Westchester, I think," she says.

"Huh," Graham says. "Not a city boy."

"Why don't you ask him about it when you all meet?" she says. "It doesn't sound like he thought he was doing anything wrong. Seems like an honest mistake. That would be interesting, don't you think? It would give you something to talk about."

Graham nods. "Maybe." He doesn't tell Carolyn but truthfully, he doesn't think it would be interesting at all. He doesn't think anything good ever came from a married man gazing at a photograph of a woman who wasn't his wife, and, if he were in Hutch's shoes—whoever he mistook the photo of Joan for—he wouldn't want to be asked about it by her husband.

"But I don't know," Graham says. "Seems asked and answered to me. I wouldn't want to embarrass the man for indulging in memories. I think if he had a private reminiscence, we should just let it lie."

Carolyn stands up and squeezes his shoulder. "Okay, Dad," she says and smiles at him. "Sorry Brett was such a pain in the ass about it. I swear I never know from one minute to the next what that kid will want to talk about and for how long."

17

The Saturday after Thanksgiving, Hutch and Alice stop at Whole Foods on their way to Julia's.

"Just let me pop in and pick up some things," Alice says. "Some good cheese and nibbles. A nice bottle of wine. I don't want to show up empty-handed."

When they get to Julia's and she opens the door, it sounds like there's already a party underway inside.

"Hey Mom, Dad, hi, come on in," she says. Julia kisses them both, her mother first. She takes their coats. "Carolyn's dad, Graham is here. Remember I told you he was coming for the week? We decided last minute to throw together a little party for all of us. Everyone's in the living room. Fun, right?"

"I didn't know that." Hutch stops and looks at his daughter. "Did you tell us that? I thought it was just going to be us." He holds up the bag from Whole Foods with the bread, cheese and wine like it will solve everything.

Julia speaks to him like he is slow. "No, I know Dad. I said it was last-minute. I didn't think anyone would mind." She looks from her mother to her father and back to her mother again. "Carolyn and I just came up with the idea like a half hour ago."

"All right then," Hutch says. "Sounds great." This is the last place in the world he wants to be.

"Wonderful," says Alice. "How lovely, sweetie."

Hutch follows his daughter and wife into the large kitchen and then away from them to a spot of clear counter space, puts down the grocery bag, and starts pulling out the contents. He pours himself a glass of wine from a bottle already opened.

"Hutch." Alice is suddenly next to him. "What was that about in the foyer?"

He looks at her and takes a sip of wine. "Sorry. I just thought it was going to be us. Honestly Alice, it's not a big deal. I'm not really up for a party and I just wasn't expecting anyone else."

"It's fine, love." Alice smiles and cocks her head defensively. "It's what, only three other people? Why that would even be a thing is surprising to me. This is Julia's dearest friend."

"I'm a surprise to myself all the time," says Hutch. "It's fine, Alice." He kisses her on the cheek and walks toward the living room where all of them are visiting. Graham is sitting in an overstuffed chair next to the fireplace. Jack is putting another log on the fire.

God help me, he thinks. *Let's get this over with.*

"Hello, Graham, is it?" Hutch says. He extends his hand and Graham stands and takes it and they shake. "Our daughters are very good friends from what I hear, for which I'm grateful. That's not an easy thing to come by I've found, so I'm glad they have such a lovely community here. Julia calls Carolyn her *framily*." He laughs.

"I'm Hutch. It's a pleasure to meet you. Happy Thanksgiving." He lifts his glass. "Long trip from New York?" He takes a deep sip.

"It's a trip I've made many, many times and it's well worth it so every time it gets shorter, or so it seems, so not so bad," says Graham. "It's good to meet you, Hutch. Happy Thanksgiving. We had a good one, how was yours?"

And it ends up being manageable. Hutch talks to Carolyn and Palmer the most, waiting—fearing—for Carolyn to bring up her son finding him holding the framed photo of Joan, which she doesn't, although he's ready to tell the same lie to this roomful of people using a different made-up name since Alice knows he never dated a woman with the same name as his grandmother. Maybe, he thinks, the kid didn't find it worth mentioning and he's grateful the boy's not there to bring it up himself and repeat his offer of internet sleuthing to help find her. The adults are here at Julia's and all four boys are next door at Carolyn's watching a movie and he expects he and Alice will leave before his grandsons come home. They were all together just two days ago, and as much as he loves Henry and Caden, he needs a fully charged battery to spend quality time with them. Tonight he is running on empty.

Graham produces a bottle of bourbon and offers a glass to anyone who wants one and Jack, Palmer, Carolyn and Hutch all take him up on it. And as Hutch settles into the cheerful, post-holiday ambiance among these friends, and his wife and daughter, and the bourbon goes to work and starts loosening his anxiety, he is tempted to engage with Graham and ask him about himself, but he knows he's incapable of it. Hutch can take this charade only so far. But as he begins feeling bolder, the lure of manipulating the conversation so that Hutch can casually share that his grandmother lived at the same address as Graham becomes so great that after an hour, he tells Alice he's got a splitting headache, and would she mind if they left.

Alice drives home and Hutch congratulates himself on managing through it so well. He's relieved it's over and grateful that he'll never be forced to spend an evening with Graham again.

18

In early November, Anne won the 23andMe kit in a raffle at her children's school's annual auction. Anne and her husband Eric attended, as they did every year, with their friends Kevin and Jessica, whose daughter Jane was best friends with Anne's oldest daughter, Katie. Now sixth graders, the girls had been inseparable since kindergarten.

Anne wrote catalog copy for the live auction items (all parents were required to donate volunteer hours toward the auction effort), but there were never any big-ticket items that she and Eric wanted to budget for or go in on with other parents. Instead, Anne and Eric bid on silent auction items they could justify the expense for—golf paraphernalia, and gorgeous homemade quilts a mother from another class donated every year. The wine wall always offered a nice selection to choose from. And there were the easel items; experiences Katie and their younger daughter, Libby, could sign up for. Every year the same two families hosted "Pixar, Pajamas, Popcorn and Pizza," in the school gym on a Saturday night in January, which was one of most popular activities, and one of the first to sell out.

The raffle tickets were ten dollars and Anne bought five. It was a painless way to contribute and something she didn't even care about winning. Anne's friend Shannon and her siblings had all done the kits and she convinced Anne that there were really fascinating things to find out: traits you wouldn't imagine you could inherit (fear of heights, photic sneeze reflex), your ethnicity percentages and distant relatives, second and third cousins like you wouldn't believe. It was staggering what a simple vial of spit could reveal.

Anne also bought two twenty-dollar tickets for the iPad raffle; she put all the stubs in her wallet and forgot about them. So when the raffles were drawn and her name was announced for the 23andMe kit, she was more surprised than anything. She hadn't forgotten she'd entered but doing so felt more like donating the fifty dollars to the school than placing a bet to win something.

She told Carolyn about it when they talked a few days later.

"Well, have you done it yet?" Carolyn asked.

"I'm not sure I care that much," Anne said. "I was really hoping for the iPad."

"You already have an iPad," said Carolyn.

"Yeah, but it's ancient, and so, so slow," said Anne. "And don't we already know everything we need to about who and where we came from? Western Europe and mostly Ireland, right? There's not much speculation with Cavanaugh, is there? And honestly, I'm a little skeptical. How reliable are these things?" Anne said.

"I know it's *scientific*—" she mocked the word. "But I just mail it off and who's even at the other end analyzing all the samples people send in?"

Carolyn laughed. "It's not a palm reading, Anne," she said. "Julia did one a few months ago. Just what she expected. Her father came from a pretty big family, so she's related to a bunch of cousins she's never heard of."

"All right, fine. Hey, why don't you do one, too?" Anne said. "Maybe we'll find some of our own cousins on there. It could be fun."

★ ★ ★

It's only the first week of December but the Christmas decorations have probably already been up in the hospital for weeks. Anne is sitting in the waiting room of the breast cancer center waiting to be called for her mammogram. It's been fourteen months since her last one, which is the first time she'd gone over the twelve-month mark between appointments.

She stores her possessions, except for her phone, in the locker the technician gave her and says yes, thank you, to an offer for a heated gown. Relaxing music is playing over the sound system and video of verdant riverbanks and trickling streams flowing over rocks loops on the big screen in the common waiting area. *It's not a spa, for God's sake, why try to pass it off as one?*

This is what Anne thinks every time she has a mammogram, but hey, she gets it. If there's any way to sweeten the experience of getting your breasts mashed between two pieces of plastic before hearing the doctor may want to speak with you before you leave, then of course there has to be some effort put in to temper the anxiety and possibility of bad news. But for Anne this diagnostic tool is a necessity and potential life saver so she would be here anyway—she'd have to be—even without the lure and illusion of comfort and calm on the way in.

Her phone pings and she glances at her email. It's from 23andMe with the subject line *Your reports are ready.*

"Anne, are you ready?"

Anne looks up at the smiling technician.

"I'm Leslie, and I'll be doing your mammogram today," says the technician. "How are you?"

Anne turns off her phone's screen and walks toward the technician. "I'm fine, thank you."

When Anne gets home, the house is empty, Eric and the girls are still at work and school. She has forty-five minutes until she needs to pick up Katie and Libby. She sits down at the computer and opens the email from 23andMe.

There's a graphic of an invitation slipping out of an open envelope with a pink and green pair of overlapping chromosomes at the top next to *23andMe*. The invitation says, *Anne, welcome to you!* Underneath that is written, *The 23andMe results for Anne Cavanaugh are in. A world of DNA discovery is waiting.* She clicks on the hot button, *View your reports*, and logs into her account.

She clicks on the Ancestry & Traits tab; under it are more choices than she expected. Ancestry & Traits Overview, All Ancestry Reports, Ancestry Composition, DNA Relatives, Traits. She clicks on Ancestry Composition. *No surprise here.* Almost eighty percent British and Irish, a little over five percent French and German, but also interesting, fifteen percent Italian and almost three percent Scandinavian. *We really are mutts*, Anne thinks.

She doesn't know if Carolyn has done her kit yet. She doubts it, Carolyn may have even forgotten about it after Anne talked to her after the auction. Life was busy enough anyway but with their father spending Thanksgiving in Portland, Carolyn had more important things to do last month. She'll find out.

She clicks on DNA Relatives, just beneath the Ancestry Composition. The name on the first line is not one she recognizes, Julia Hutchinson. *Half-sister.* Carolyn's name is not listed.

"What?" Anne says aloud to an empty room.

Below Julia Hutchinson's name are other names Anne doesn't recognize: first cousins once and twice removed, second, third and fourth cousins. The lists of these relatives go on for thirty pages. She looks back at the details under half-sister: nearly twenty-three percent DNA shared, fifty-three segments. She clicks on Julia's name, a hot link which takes Anne to Julia's profile.

She reads: *Your genetic relationship. You and Julia likely share one parent who gave each of you a different mix of their DNA.* Beneath that, strangely, is a rudimentary family tree diagram illustrating how Parent, You and Half-Sister are related, as if someone who couldn't read the words communicating such unexpected news needed the graphic version to understand it.

Anne looks at the information under Julia's name: Female. Birth Year: 1970. Location: Portland, Oregon, United States.

Anne thinks, *Julia Hutchinson is five years younger than me and lives in the same city as my sister. She is the same age as Carolyn.*

She dials Carolyn's number.

"Hey," says Carolyn.

"Can you talk?"

"Sure, what's up? Your appointment was today, right? Everything okay?"

"Yes, well, yeah, with the mammo, everything's fine," says Anne. "But I did that kit I won at the auction, the 23andMe thing, and I got the results today. I hope you're sitting down. Jesus. We have a half-sister. Carolyn, I think Dad had an affair."

19

By late afternoon the next day, Ceci and Anne and Carolyn have talked multiple times, and Carolyn and Julia have talked multiple times, and Julia has logged into her 23andMe profile and sent Anne a note, and Julia has talked to Alice and Hutch, and Hutch has broken down. Anne, incredulous, understands that Graham is not her biological father. No one has spoken to Graham.

And then, she thinks, how in the world will they tell him? Anne's heartbreak at the truth she knows now, she imagines, will only pale in comparison to Graham's. After all this time, so many years after he and Joan raised their daughters together, and such a long time after losing his wife, is it something he needs to know? Do they have to tell him?

It's different for Anne—the biological aspect is important, Joan's choice affects her own children, too—but for Graham there is no such benefit, nothing to be gained, and no way for him to reconcile with Joan now, and no way for Joan to explain if she wanted to or make amends, as she surely would need to, with all of them.

When she was fifteen, Anne and her mother had gotten in an argument that not only had Anne never forgotten, but it was one that as she got older and made certain choices, made her realize that both she and Joan—if Joan remembered the argument as well—could look back and each realize what Joan had said came true because of what Joan accurately predicted, or had *become* true precisely because what Joan said had provided Anne with a suggestion, or an invitation to follow.

Although Anne remembers the argument, and the words they'd exchanged, she only vaguely remembers the issue that sparked the problem in the first place: wanting to stay with a friend instead of going away for a family weekend with friends of her parents.

"I don't know any other way to say this," Joan said. "I wish there were another one I could think of, and I'm sorry about it, but there isn't."

"Say what?" Anne said. "Mom, for God's sake whatever is it just spit it out. You've already told me you're pissed. What's one more thing?"

"You're selfish," Joan said. "And I hate saying it, Anne, I really do, but you need to hear it. You are. You're selfish and one day you're just going to move away and leave this family behind and just not have anything to do with us. Just not look back."

"Oh my God," said Anne. "That's what *you* think of my wanting to not go on one stupid weekend away with the ridiculous Thompson family because I have other plans? That I'm selfish?"

"Okay, okay," Joan said. She held up her hands and wagged her palms at Anne. "That's enough. I don't care to hear the weekend is stupid and there's no reason to be unkind about the Thompsons. They're very fond of all you girls. But this is what I'm talking about. You can't muster some generosity, some selflessness to spend a weekend with our family and theirs, as if it's such a huge sacrifice, so enormous, that it's an impossible one for you to make. So far, you've been able to do whatever you want every other weekend this summer. It's one goddamn weekend, Anne. You do realize, there's not very much that you're asked to do around here that you don't want to do."

And so, after she graduated from college and took a job with a magazine that moved her to Italy, Anne freshly recalled the argument. As thrilled as Joan was, because she knew how excited Anne was—and proud, too; it was a coveted position—Anne thought, *Mom, I guess you were right. Really, what did you expect?*

And now today, she thinks, *You were selfish, too. Who knew we had that in common?*

20

What a surprise to have all my girls together and back home! Graham thinks.

Carolyn and Anne are coming in on the same flight from Chicago and Ceci is driving down from Boston and picking them up at the airport on her way to have Christmas with him a few weeks early. They all have such busy lives and families, it's never easy for even one of them to get away for a visit without planning in advance. He's amazed the three of them coordinated to pull it off.

Their spontaneous visit is unexpected, but not unwelcome, and Graham asks Lois, who cleans the apartment every month, if she can squeeze him in between her other scheduled cleanings to do a quick spruce up of the place, and she manages it. Although she charges him her regular fee, his generous tip doubles it. Since it was just going to be him, he hadn't planned on getting a tree, but he goes out and gets a good one and puts only the lights on. The four of them can hang the rest of the decorations together. He buys a wreath for the front door. He always sends the three of them Christmas cards with checks for everyone in their families, but this year he'll be able to give them in person. He stocks the fridge and buys enough bottles of wine to get a discount.

When his daughters get to the apartment a little after six, Graham is reminded of them as little girls, coming home from school together at the end of the day, tumbling into the house like puppies. He realizes this is the first time all three of them have been here together as adults without boyfriends, fiancés, spouses or children. Immediately he is struck by the sense that in addition to their trips to get here, the three of them have coordinated some type of rehearsed situation, what he can't imagine, but he knows his daughters well enough to see the pattern. He's seen it before for surprise birthday and anniversary parties.

Only in hindsight, of course, but once it's happened multiple times, he can detect their tells: For one, both Anne and Carolyn defer to Ceci. Although she is the oldest, she is also the most dominating when a plan needs to be pulled off and she naturally occupies the role of the person running the show, as she does tonight after they've gotten settled, and the girls have opened wine and put out crackers and cheese and a dish of nuts.

Then, Anne and Carolyn, like foot soldiers in lockstep, are waiting in the wings to be called upon, sitting on the smaller couch. Carolyn seems to have shrunken into herself, holding her wine glass tightly, and Anne, sitting next to her, with her right leg crossed over her left and bouncing her right foot idly, has given herself a generous pour. And Graham thinks, *Anne does not look happy. Ceci and Carolyn do not look happy either.*

But as Graham sits down on the larger couch across from them, and Ceci takes a seat next to him, he breaks into their script, disrupting whatever was going to come next. Clearly something is going on, there is a problem or a situation that they are in the midst of, and he is here, their father is here, and whatever it is, he will help them sort it out.

"Is someone getting divorced?" he says. "Or are we dealing with breast cancer? Or is it another diagnosis?"

"Oh, Dad," Ceci says. She shakes her head and reaches out to touch his hand. Now, Graham thinks, she doesn't look so much unhappy as unbearably sad.

Remarkably, Anne refills her empty wine glass.

"Dad, I did one of those 23andMe DNA kits last month," Anne says. "Something I won at the kids' school auction. When I got the results, well, what I found out was upsetting. I have a half-sister. At first, we were all worried you had an affair."

"What you found out," Graham says. He has heard the words that Anne just said, but as soon as she finishes talking, he tries to remember them. They seem irretrievable, like a conversation between two strangers he was eavesdropping on but who have since walked away so he has only heard the beginning of the story.

"This is very difficult, Dad," Anne says. "You're not my father."

Graham feels like he is standing at the end of a long, dark tunnel. He focuses on breathing deeply, feeling his feet on the floor beneath him, feeling his body on the couch that's supporting his weight, his body, all the years of his life. The cumulative experiences we have are contained in our bodies, he thinks. We're each our own suitcase carrying them all around, year after year, until the suitcase isn't meant to hold or carry any more experiences and our lives end.

He can feel his daughters—ah, but one of them is not his daughter—looking at him, and at each other, also breathing, and waiting, afraid and worried and sorry and anxious.

"Oh, God," he says into his knees, gazing at the living room rug. "I was afraid of this. I'm so sorry, Anne."

There is a moment of quiet that feels theatrical, that goes on longer than it should, and Graham wishes he could take back the words he's just uttered.

"What do you mean?" Anne says, just above a whisper. "Did you know? How much fucking worse is this fiasco that is my life going to get?"

Graham walks over to the other couch and says, "May I please sit down?"

Carolyn walks to the other couch and sits down next to Ceci and Graham takes Carolyn's place next to Anne.

"No, no, I'm sorry," says Graham. "Let me explain." He picks up Anne's hand, which she tries to pull away, but Graham grasps it tighter. "No darling, please don't do that. Listen, please?"

And Anne surrenders her hand to Graham.

"There was a period of time when I was in law school and Ceci was a baby that I suspected your mother might have been unfaithful for a time, but I was a coward and didn't confront her. I didn't want to know the truth, and she never hinted that she wanted to leave me, so I fooled myself into believing whatever had happened—if anything had—was short-lived and had no lasting repercussions. We went on to have two more children and were married for almost thirty years. That's not nothing. And during that time when I was suspicious, I was honestly not a very good husband so part of my keeping quiet was to eliminate any opportunity for your mother to share her unhappiness about me with me.

"So, no, I didn't know this about you Anne, truly, but your telling me about this test confirms not only what I was afraid of, but something far more serious."

He drops Anne's hand and puts his arm around her and pulls her toward him.

Graham's eyes start to fill. "I am so very sorry. And your life is not a fiasco, darling. It's a gift, just like you, and we'll figure it out. We'll figure everything out together. I'm still your father. That has not changed."

And Carolyn and Ceci walk to the kitchen to leave the two of them alone as Anne cries against him.

21

Christmas is a week away and Carolyn and Julia haven't spoken in ten days. Carolyn has texted and left voicemails, before and after going to see Graham and nothing. If Julia freezing her out has something to do with Anne, Carolyn can't understand why.

She is cleaning out closets to make a Goodwill run. She's in the guest room closet where the least worn, most out-of-style coats live, saved for the rare times they're worn to shovel snow or rake leaves. The cleaning out is long overdue.

There's a purple (what was she thinking?) Patagonia fleece that Carolyn had forgotten about and has since replaced with two newer generations of coats that she wears often. She takes it off the hanger to put in the donate bag and checks the pockets. Nothing in the small zippered one on the sleeve or the right one, but in the left one she feels a small piece of paper. She pulls it out and is surprised it's something that's been there all this time, the ticket stub for the first movie she and Julia had ever seen together, *In the Bedroom*. They both loved it and were both surprised on Oscar night when it didn't win Best Picture.

How had she come home from the movies that night (again, had she really worn this purple fleece?) and just left the ticket stub in there for all this time? It was the beginning of their just becoming friends; they had seen the movie downtown and had a glass of wine afterward.

"Goddamn it," she says. She pulls her phone out of her back pocket, takes a picture of the ticket and texts it to Julia. *Look what I found.* She watches the screen and sees the floating dots, then nothing.

This is fucking ridiculous, she thinks.

Carolyn knows Julia is home; her car is there, and Carolyn has seen Julia in her kitchen. Instead of knocking on the front door, she walks, familiarly, into her backyard, the way they always go into each other's houses, taps on the back door and goes into the kitchen.

Julia is unloading the dishwasher and turns around. She smiles and shakes her head at Carolyn like she is ignoring a child throwing a tantrum.

"Wow, you don't get the message, so you just walk through my back fucking door?" Julia said. "You're a therapist, so boundaries, right?"

"Don't do that," Carolyn says. "I've called, texted, nothing. What is going on Julia? I don't know why you're shutting me out. I didn't sleep with your father."

"Wow," says Julia. "That was uncalled for."

"I'm sorry, but you've got to help me out here," Carolyn says. "I seriously don't understand."

Julia sighs. "She was just so fucking *wonderful,* your mother, that's always been your refrain, Carolyn. 'Wonderful, dead, beloved and so dearly missed Joan.' And really, this, *this* is who she was. Not so wonderful at all. A liar, someone who kept something so important an iron clad secret for her whole life. Her whole life! Can you imagine? Could you imagine keeping losing your daughters a secret?"

"That's not fair, and a different thing entirely," Carolyn says. "But what good does it do for you to cut me off? Times were different, it was fifty years ago. I don't know, they were young, she was unhappy, my father was an asshole then. Maybe she didn't know."

"Honestly," says Julia. "She had to know. Now I have a half-sister, your sister. I need a break. I need to not be with you, talking to you all the time about this, especially before she and I meet. It's just too much and hard to explain. Try to understand. Our relationship has changed. I just need a little space."

2015

22

Graham flies to Portland, again, in early January and he stops his mind from going to a precious place about Joan during take-off. Instead, he talks to his seatmate, a new mother flying by herself for the first time with her baby who is five months old and crying. Her husband is already there for a conference and the two of them are joining him before they all go to Hawaii.

He's going to Portland for one purpose this time, to meet with Peter Hutchinson, a situation he never imagined confronting. His worst fears about Joan did not include this fact about Anne. For this trip he's staying at The Benson, a historic downtown Portland hotel, with a 4.5-star rating. He hasn't told any of the girls he's making the trip; maybe he'll tell them after the fact, and maybe he won't. Although at some point he will have to set the tone about how they'll move forward, whatever those many ways will be, and no path will be the wrong one, he's already prepared to say.

This meeting is necessary, and Hutch knows it, and told Graham as much over text.

I suppose we need to talk about it all, Hutch texted. *I can come to you, too.*

No, I'll make the trip, Graham responded. He doesn't want Hutch in his house. The very place where it all happened.

Now, they are on the rooftop patio of The Indigo, where Hutch and Alice live, sipping Four Roses bourbon around one of the propane fire pits.

Graham sits across from this man, who is Anne's father, this man he now knows he has run into before, decades ago, this man who just two months ago he met properly for the first time.

"Graham," Hutch says. "Thank you for coming. I have to say, from the start, I'm so sorry. I really am so very, very sorry."

Graham shakes his head. "I don't know what's to be said or done about it now," he says. "But you knew who I was at Thanksgiving, Jesus Christ."

"If you were me, what would you have said or done?" Hutch says. "It goes without saying that night was very difficult to get through."

"Oh fuck you." Graham says. "The only reason I'm here is for you to look me in the eye and tell me why you slept with my wife. We had a baby. What the fuck was wrong with you?"

"It's not complicated. I was young, and I was in love," Hutch says. "I was in love with her. She was my first love."

"She was mine, too," says Graham.

"I wanted you to see this," says Hutch. "It's a letter I received a very long time ago from a man name Peter Herring letting me know she had died." He hands Graham the letter. "I guess she didn't tell him the whole story," Hutch says. "She wanted me to know she was gone, but nothing else."

Graham reads it and hands it back to Hutch and takes a deep sip from his glass.

"That's really something, that Peter did what she asked him to. I remember that Christmas so well," Graham says. "You have no idea. Like it was yesterday. You know she wore the most incredible green dress during that visit. I mean it. I can close my eyes and see her and Peter playing chess, as they often did when he and Anne were together. That dress was Joan's favorite and even then, after all the chemo and radiation, she looked exquisite in it. I really thought she would beat it. I thought she was going to beat the fucking thing."

"I am sorry about that, too," says Hutch. "She was so young."

"It's remarkable to me that the girls are older than she ever was," Graham says. "Strange."

"She never would have left you, you know," says Hutch. "And she knew I knew that. Maybe I'm stating the obvious, but I think it's worth saying. Something you should know. That's why I ended it. We were just two lonely people who kept each other company for a while but I was chasing my tail. There wasn't ever going to be anything more between us."

"You ended it?" Graham says. "Did you know she was pregnant?"

"No, and at that point I don't know if she knew either," says Hutch. "But I don't think that would have made a difference. I wouldn't have doubted you were the father. And I'm confident she never would have told me the truth. All of it was on Joan's terms, and I'm willing to bet that she would have ended it when she found out she was pregnant."

Hutch gives them each another pour.

"Two lonely people," Graham says. "How very sad. She was married for Christ's sake. But to tell you the truth, at that time I was terribly remiss at being her husband."

"You know my grandmother wanted the three of us to meet, all have lunch together. She thought you were a nice couple I should be friends with," Hutch says. "She lived on the eighth floor and introduced Joan and me when we all ran into each other in the park one day. But I had seen her months earlier at D'Agostino's, crazy snowstorm that day. We were in the same check-out line."

"I remember that storm. What a brutal winter. I was in bed with the flu," says Graham, "otherwise she never would have gone out in that. She left the apartment as soon as she put Ceci down for a nap. I was sick for a week."

"Huh. Is that so?" Hutch says, barely.

"I remember your grandmother," Graham says. "She was a neat lady."

"She was. We were very close," says Hutch. "What in the world would she make of all this?"

"Can you imagine," Graham says.

They drink in silence.

"What does Alice think?" says Graham.

"She knew about Joan, the merest facts, nothing more. I don't think she would ever say it, but I'm sure she's disappointed in me," Hutch says. "I think she's mostly concerned about Anne, and Julia. She's a good mother and knows this has to be a difficult thing to come to terms with."

"You're a lucky man," Graham says.

"Mostly, that's true," says Hutch. "But not as lucky as I could have been. Our son died when he was seventeen. In a car accident the night of his high school graduation."

And Hutch tells him the story again.

23

Alice was determined that Hutch didn't know she was upset. It was one thing for them all to find out at the same time about Anne, but it was another entirely that Hutch had never uttered more than this to Alice about Joan, when they were newly married, in love and sharing romantic histories: *It was back when I had just graduated college and was spending a lot of time with my grandmother. I met a woman and hoped it might develop into something, but it wasn't meant to be.* Nothing about that woman being married or having a child.

Alice had told Hutch about her college sweetheart Frank and how crushed she was that he never proposed, went into a lot of detail honestly—maybe more than Hutch wanted to know—about her heartbreak over a certainty she believed in that simply didn't materialize and never would.

But when Alice pressed him, "What was her name?" "Why wasn't it meant to be?" Hutch had just looked at her with a sad expression and said, "What does it matter, that's the beginning and end of the story, there's nothing more to say."

Feeling both scolded and strangely combative, Alice said, "Okay, we can forget about it Hutch. It's not that I want you to share anything you don't want to, *with the woman you're married to*, but this is about you, someone who was important to you, a significance in your life, and you're the one I'm interested in, you. But fine, let's drop it."

That was decades ago.

So now, with the existence of Anne indicating there was far, far more to the story, it felt too late for Alice to still be curious, open, vulnerable, complicit even, in her husband's past. It was literally there in black and white: *My name is Anne Cavanaugh and a 23andMe kit indicates we may be related. I got your email address from Julia. I'm sure this is unexpected but when you can please let me know how/when we may connect.*

Alice had looked over her glasses, and had seen Hutch, in his immediate shock, first stare at the screen, frozen, before abruptly start to laugh the soundless hysteria that can't be stopped with threats or reason, before just as abruptly silently begin to weep, tears streaming down both cheeks. If she hadn't been across the room and able to see him, she would have had no idea he was doing anything besides the crossword.

After Hutch said, *Alice, can you please come here and read this,* and showed her the email, she made the conscious, cold, unloving choice to pivot, turn her back on him, and walk back to her chair and resume the needlepoint she'd been working on mere minutes before.

She focused on her breathing to quiet her shaking hands and reeling mind. She had read somewhere about breathing a certain way to manage panic: inhale for eight seconds, exhale for ten, or was it the other way around?

No shaking hands, slow down the needle. Look at the pattern. Breathe—am I at in or out? Stop. Breathe in for ten, hold—just hold the needle, don't try a stitch right now—then out for eight. Slowly. Okay that worked. Let's do that again. Stop. Just put down the needle. Lay it on the canvas. I am across the room, Hutch can't see me, he's not looking anyway. Breathe again, in, hold, then out.

We have been through much, much worse. Marriage is about forgiveness and the desire to stay together being stronger, much stronger, than the desire to walk away.

It's not that he knew and didn't tell me.

So why am I acting like he kept something from me.

Because he did.

They were alone in it together for the time being. He was alone and she was alone, and they had been here before. So much worse than this.

In their marriage they have each had the ability to soften when the other needed it. After Mark.

She breathed and put down the needlepoint and crossed the room and while Hutch was still silently weeping, she knelt in front of him and wrapped her arms around his neck, pulling his head onto her shoulder. "Hutch," she said, "it's us. We're okay. Are you okay?"

"I'm sorry," he said, gasping. "I'm just so sorry. I never knew."

They'll get through it. She must get through this shock. When she can, she will take another stitch in the needlepoint, then another and another. She will figure out how to talk to her husband. She will ask him what he wants to do now that he knows he is Anne Cavanaugh's father.

24

The next week, Anne is flying from Chicago to Portland to meet Hutch (she's constantly grappling with the words, *birth father)*, Alice, and Julia, in this new context. August five years ago was the last time she, Eric and their girls traveled to Portland, and Carolyn and Anne had gone in together and rented a house in Manzanita at the Oregon Coast for ten days. During that trip Anne had met Julia only briefly. When she recalls that visit, the idea of sitting down with the three of them now knowing Julia is not merely Carolyn's neighbor makes Anne feel sick. Eric insisted on making the trip with her, but Anne told him she wanted to do it alone.

It's okay, she told him. *I'll call and fill you in. It's just a couple days anyway. I don't want the girls' schedules disrupted.*

To distract herself, she considers how Julia and Carolyn might repair their friendship. *Shouldn't it be stronger now?* She thinks. *I will do what I can.* She'll try to bring Julia and Carolyn back together, try to help mitigate the displaced anger Julia has toward Joan, a woman she never met. She will try to reconcile this new truth about herself with the fact that Graham is still her father, and that her mother was flawed, but mostly a good one. But Anne has no idea what she'll do with all her own anger.

She knows she has to be the connective tissue, the healing bond between all these people. And she can only do so much.

And now there's also Alice. While Anne won't be looking to her to replace Joan, Alice can become a friend and it can only improve the situation if Anne gets to know her.

Five years after Joan's death, Graham had bought each of them a copy of *Motherless Daughters,* as soon as it came out, simultaneously proud and shy, inscribing the same thing in all three books:

With any luck you girls will have me for a long time to come, but this book is very popular, and I don't doubt will be helpful in ways that I never can be. Much love, Dad.

And Graham had been right, not the least of which for all three of them was knowing that there were so very many women of all ages, especially young ones, who were enduring the same void they were, and for that alone, the book, and Graham's gesture, had been a great comfort. Maybe getting to know Alice can offer the same kind of help that book did, Anne thinks.

She has been texting Carolyn since she left for the airport, obsessing about the impression she'll make when she meets Hutch, Alice and Julia, imploring Carolyn to share what she thinks. Anne has sent four texts:

Am I doing the right thing?
Would you be doing this?
I'm afraid Julia will resent me. What do you think?
What is Alice like?

And in response to each text Anne has seen the three engagement dots, then nothing except for the two responses Carolyn has sent.

I think you're the only one who knows if this is right. It's right if it's right for you.

I have no idea how Julia will respond. We're not speaking.

★ ★ ★

Anne is drunk and texts Carolyn from the Uber. *Pulling up to your house, let me in please!*

The driver lets her out and as the car pulls away, Anne shouts, "Thank you! Have a good night!"

Carolyn is standing on the porch. "Hey, sis!" Anne says, and waves.

"Where are you coming from?" Carolyn says. "Julia lives right next door." She points to the house.

"Someplace," Anne says. "Some dark, fancy, fucking place. Downton, sorry," she laughs. "I mean *downtown!* Downtown. I drank too much, and I had to leave. They're such nice people!"

"Yes, they are," says Carolyn. "They're nice people."

Anne sits down on the couch in the living room and Carolyn brings her a glass of water and sits next to her.

Anne looks at the photo of Joan on the mantel and starts to laugh. "Why did she do it, Carolyn? Why the fuck didn't she tell me? A deathbed is the ideal place for sharing that kind of thing. Honestly, custom made." She holds up both hands in an elaborate okay gesture.

"I don't know," says Carolyn. "I'm wondering the same thing."

"I deserved to know, goddamn it," Anne says. "This impacts my children, too. She was a goddamn liar; my whole life was a lie."

"I think it's safe to say that she thought we'd never find out," Carolyn says. "It was a risky gamble, obviously."

"You know Julia and Hutch and I all sneeze when we look at the sun?" Anne says. "It's genetic. Her brother, Mark, he used to, too. You don't. Nobody else in the family does. Billy Joel is my favorite musician and he's Hutch's, too. 'Scenes from an Italian Restaurant' tops both our lists. Isn't that so fucking weird?"

"It's weird, I guess. But do you think after a little time that things might go back to mostly the way they were?" Carolyn says. "I mean your family is still your family. I'm sure any genetic information is helpful but it's not like you have a whole new family, is it?"

"I don't know," Anne says. "I have to figure that out. I like them, but it's all so fucked up. I'll tell you one thing though, it's back to therapy for me."

Carolyn sighs. "I hope you have a good therapist. We all probably should."

"At least you're well connected," Anne says.

"Yeah, well," Carolyn says. "It's not like we all know each other."

"What if she didn't know?" Anne says. "I mean it's a terrible thing she did, keeping a secret like that, but she had to know, right? I have two children and I've been pregnant three times, and every time I knew exactly when it happened. Didn't you?"

"Yeah," Carolyn says. "Pretty much."

"Unless she was fucking both of them on the same day, every day," Anne says. "Which I would find hard to believe and don't even want to think about. But I wouldn't have thought she'd fuck someone else, either. Who even was she?"

"She was a person and a woman, not just our mother," Carolyn says. "And people are complicated, and they make mistakes. God knows you and I both have."

"I didn't want to start therapy tonight, with you," Anne says. "Jesus."

"Yeah, you couldn't pay me enough," says Carolyn.

"I told Julia to talk to you, by the way," Anne says, and waves her hand. "She'll be fine, you guys will be fine. You're right there for her to take things out on but it'll be okay."

"And you'll be okay, too, Anne. We all will, I know it," Carolyn says. "Everything's going to be okay."

"Mom used to say that all the time, didn't she?" says Anne. "Remember, when someone was troubled or ruffled about something. Always that same refrain, 'You're okay. Everything is going to be okay.' I wonder if it was really us she was talking to."

25

Hutch is certain there aren't many more selfish things that a person could do than what Joan did, keeping the truth from Anne her whole life. Keeping it from him was a far lesser moral transgression in the scheme of things, but a decision that was also selfish.

He keeps this thought in mind while he waits for Anne. She met with the three of them—him, Julia and Alice—last night, but he wants a visit alone with her, just a quick chat, before she flies back to Chicago. It feels important, necessary, to have time to say and share things that didn't feel appropriate with his wife and daughter present. His other daughter.

He's gotten a table for them at Zeus Café, a short walk from The Indigo. Maybe they'll eat lunch, maybe they won't, but at least it will be an option. And they serve drinks. He'll ask Anne if she wants a glass of wine. He's already ordered one.

Anne breezes in, seeming rushed, and Hutch stands. She sees him and walks toward the table. He waits for her to sit before he does again.

"I know we just saw each other last night," Hutch says. "A get-to-know-you, tell-me-about-your-life, describe your family, but it felt to me like going through the motions. And ones that weren't all that critical at that, although Eric and the girls do sound extraordinary. But superficial might have been the best we could all do last night. Do you want a glass or wine, or iced tea? Or something else? Order whatever you want."

"I'll have a glass of wine, thank you," says Anne. "And I have to apologize, I overdid it last night. Before I knew it, I was quite overserved. This has been, well, 'a lot,'"—she uses air quotes— "doesn't even begin to cover it. I'm sure you would agree, or at least understand." She orders a glass of wine and they tell the server they need some time.

"Do you have time for lunch?" Hutch says. "When is your flight?"

"My flight's not till seven," says Anne. "So I'm not in a hurry."

"Good," says Hutch. "Very good. Thank you again for meeting me, you know, again." He is suddenly at a loss for words. Or rather, there are too many words, too many thoughts ready to pour out of him, that he simply doesn't know where to begin. He takes a deep sip of wine and empties his glass.

"I feel a certain amount of responsibility, obviously," Hutch says. "I can't speak to your mother's actions, and what she did infuriates me, honestly. The whole course of my life may have been different. I don't know. But I am accountable for having a relationship with a married woman and I just wanted you to know that I loved her." He laughs.

"I don't think saying that would have gone over that well with last night's audience. But I want you to know that if she had left your father for me, which was never going to happen, just so you know, I would have spent the rest of my life doing everything I could to make her happy. It wasn't just a fling, not for me. I ended it because I knew she was never going to leave your father. I'm sorry that I didn't know she was pregnant before I did so. But I can't imagine I would have thought the baby was mine. Given what has happened, if I had known and I'd asked her, I'm quite certain that she would have lied to me."

"You know, my whole family, all of us, thought we knew exactly who my mother was her whole life, our whole lives," Anne says. "And to me that's even stranger, if that's possible, than the truth about my situation, our situation. It's staggering to me that we didn't have any idea who she was. And I'm angry, certainly, but in another bizarre and disorienting way, I feel like my anger is directed at a stranger. My mother, the woman I knew and loved, the woman who raised me, seems like a different person altogether, than this alternative version of her that I'm now hearing about for the first time. That probably doesn't make any sense."

Hutch lifts his hand for the server, and points to Anne's glass and she nods.

"It makes sense to me," Hutch says. "I think we're all trying to reconcile those two versions of her. I know I am. I can't imagine your father—how Graham's processing it. Listen, we don't have to dwell on it, or we can talk about it as long as you want. It's just important to me that you know, depending on how you feel or what you want, that I'm at your disposal, available. But I'm a follower here. Any kind of association you want to have with me, or my family, is up to you. You're in the lead. And know whatever you decide, my feelings won't be hurt. Whatever you want or don't, is fine with me. And there's no rush. We can figure it out.

"You know, Alice has a friend, back in New York, Betsy, and Betsy has an adult son, I can't think of his name, but he's married, has kids, he's around your age. Anyway, he— Betsy's son—was a sperm donor when he was in college. I guess that's one way to pay the bills, right? And last year he was contacted by a young lady who was the, uh, product I guess, of one of his donations. 23andMe was how she found him, too. Story was, years ago the young lady's mother was single and she wanted to have a baby and Betsy's son was the donor she went with. When Alice told me that Betsy's son—Adam, *yes!* that's his name—that Adam didn't want anything to do with this young woman, his biological daughter, I was really shocked.

"That was before our situation, and a different scenario altogether, but there are some similarities and I've been recalling how shocked I was at Adam's response. Sure, the young lady has her family, has her mother, and Adam has his family, his wife and kids but I couldn't understand the lack of compassion or humanity or just plain interest coming from Adam. I don't believe the young lady was looking for a dad. I don't know the man, maybe he has some regrets or is embarrassed, who knows. Just like us, you have your family and I have mine, but we are related, we have a connection and that's not nothing. Not to me. I'm not like Adam."

"Adam is an asshole," Anne says, and smiles. "Don't be like Adam."

"Goddamn right," says Hutch.

"And, also, by the way, don't be like Joan." Anne says. "It's crazy, years ago, when Carolyn was going through a rough time, she came up with a new acronym WWJD—*What Would Joan Do?*—you know, a play on the Bible thumpers' mantra, and for a while that was one of our family's resources for making decisions. Something I think people do when someone they still need isn't around anymore to help. And when I think back to that expression, which was funny and comforting then, it just feels like a mockery now."

Hutch winces and looks at his hands in his lap. "I can only imagine that if your mother were able to, she would express tremendous remorse. I truly believe that."

"There's no way to know." Anne shakes her head. "But I have to disagree with you. She had ample time and chances to tell me. I imagine the only remorse she would feel is for the fact that we found out."

Hutch feels like their time together, which is going better than he expected, is going off the rails in a way he also didn't expect. Immediate course correction is necessary.

"Listen, last night just didn't feel like the time to unload all that, everything I just said, and I really wanted to say it all to you in person," Hutch says. "A phone call or text, that just wouldn't have been right."

"I understand," says Anne. "Thank you, really. Please thank Alice, too. I don't know if I would be so gracious, so generous, if I were in her place."

"She's extraordinary," Hutch says. "God knows what I would do without her."

They sit quietly for a minute.

"Would you mind if we stayed a little longer?" Anne says. "I'd like to have lunch."

"Great," says Hutch. "Me, too." He looks around for the server.

"Good," she says.

Hutch is going to have lunch with his daughter. He is doing something for the first time with Anne that millions of men around the world do every day, take for granted and don't give a second thought. Certainly he has as well with Julia, countless times. *I'm meeting my daughter for lunch.*

In that moment the specific gravity of an otherwise globally insignificant statement causes a catch in his throat. What must people think as they look through the restaurant window or pass by their table, if they think anything at all? Do they see a father and daughter? Or two professionals who are grabbing a quick lunch out of the office—a mentor and his protégé? Do they believe they're catching a glimpse of two lovers who have picked a place remote and far enough from where they'd run into anyone they know? Hutch didn't realize it the night before, in dimmer lighting and with Alice and Julia to engage as well but sitting with her across the table from him today, he is struck by how strongly Anne resembles Joan.

Is this what Joan looked like in the last years of her life, before she got sick? Could Anne at the age of twenty-three have passed for Joan's twin?

Composure, he thinks, *that's what's needed here. Composure and focus.*

Hutch clasps his hands in front of him. "After last night all I know is Eric is a mortgage broker, you work at *Chicago* magazine, Katie's a sixth grader and Libby's in fourth," Hutch says. "Tell me about your life."

"Like a job interview?" Anne laughs. "Strengths and weaknesses?"

"Sure," says Hutch. "Why not? Let's see. Okay, I'll start: I've never been able to keep a houseplant alive."

Anne smiles and looks out the window. "My mother's middle name was Katherine; Katie is named after her. Eric's grandmother was Elizabeth, so Libby is a nod to her. I really wanted a big family, four or five kids, but I had Libby when I was thirty-nine and the girls were so perfect, and it just seemed like pushing our luck. Both Ceci and Carolyn have boys. Having girls is so different. I fell in love with Italy when I was in college, fell in love with a boy there too, Peter Herring, and went back and worked there after college before my mom got sick."

Hutch says he loves Italy too, that's where he and Alice spent their honeymoon. He tells Anne it was Peter who wrote to him about Joan's death.

"I remember finding the letter for him in my mother's jewelry box," says Anne. "We were just good friends by then. I never even thought to do anything except send Joan's note to him. Peter and my mother had been good friends too.

"As much as I loved Italy, after a few years I really missed my family," Anne says. "And after going through losing my mom I realized how important being closer was."

"How did you and Eric meet?" Hutch says.

"It's funny," says Anne. "We were set up on a blind date by mutual friends one summer, but after we'd gone out a few times, we realized we had been at the same New Year's Eve party earlier that year, each of us with a date. Strange, the couple that set us up is divorced now. I have no idea why. Eric and I drifted apart from them when they moved from the city to the suburbs. People changing. Oldest story in the world, right?"

Anne looks wistful and sad recalling this combination of one happy memory, and a different, more disappointing fact of her life, and Hutch realizes he'll only ever know a small portion of who Anne is. With any luck, there will be more time, they will have more chances, for him to find out as much as she's willing to share with him.

Anne smiles at him then looks over his shoulder out the window at the downtown Portland street and then down at the floor before she looks at him again. "Will you tell me about the two of you?" She says, "Tell me the story of you and Joan?"

Hutch looks at the ceiling and wipes at the corners of his eyes. He starts with his grandmother and tells Anne everything.

26

The afternoon after Anne leaves, Julia walks from her backyard into Carolyn's, knocks on the back door, and walks into the house.

"Hello?" she calls. "Anyone home?"

Carolyn is sewing in the dining room, finishing the quilt. She stops the machine and walks into the kitchen.

"Hey, what's up?" she says, and crosses her arms.

Julia holds up the bottle of wine she's brought. "Olive branch," she says. "How about a glass?"

They take glasses and the bottle to the dining room and Julia admires the quilt on the way. "Wow, it's incredible, really. Brooke is going to love it." Brooke is Carolyn's pregnant colleague who has an office next to hers.

They sit down and Julia opens the bottle and pours. "The last time you and I did this together feels like a whole lifetime ago," she says. "I've really missed you."

"I've missed you, too," Carolyn says. "Anne just left yesterday."

"Yeah, I know," says Julia. "We've been in touch."

"Right," says Carolyn.

"Listen, I know it's been a while and I'm sorry," Julia says. "It was weird to not do Christmas with you. I have gifts for everyone."

"You wanted space," Carolyn says. "And I gave it to you for like a fucking month. That's such a long time I just assumed our friendship was over. Awkward with the whole next-door thing but I was getting used to it. You know it's not just your life that was turned upside down. And besides all of that, you were the one I wanted to talk to about my best friend not talking to me, so I've been feeling especially alone."

"I know, and I really am sorry," says Julia. "I wasn't even sure you'd let me in if I came over it's been so long, and I've been an asshole. So can I explain?"

"Go ahead," Carolyn says.

"You know after Mark died, for the rest of high school I would fantasize about belonging to a different family. Remember on *The Brady Bunch* how Oliver moved in with their family?" says Julia. "I would have loved an arrangement like that. Just a whole household of new people. It was better when I went to college because the playing field was level. People didn't know what happened unless I told them."

"You never told me that," Carolyn says.

"It didn't seem relevant," says Julia. "But the other thing that I did later without realizing it at first, is I gravitated toward people who had some kind of trauma or loss. I wouldn't even know it at first, just people I hit it off with and made friends with easily would end up having a sad story or struggle of their own. I hit the jackpot with you."

Carolyn smiles and nods. "Yeah, I know what you mean."

"That's not the basis of our friendship but we share, I guess, a sensibility, that people who haven't experienced that just don't possess," Julia says. "That word *framily* we always throw around so easily. And now, we're not related to each other, but we are both equally related to the same person. It's kind of a mindfuck. Especially since I always imagined having that other family. Now I do literally have Anne to explore a relationship with, in addition to what I have with you. Anne and I are the same as you and Anne. I just needed time to process it. And I saw someone to get some help with all of it. She doesn't know you."

Carolyn laughs. "That's what I told Anne. It's not a club."

"Anyway, I really am sorry," Julia says. "I hope we can find a way to be okay again."

"We will," Carolyn says. "Don't worry about that. I'm not going anywhere."

"There's just one more thing," says Julia. "And this is harder for me to say. People are always a little bit canonized after they die, I think, you know? Revered and considered infallible in a way that we don't when people are still alive. And I did that with Joan, vicariously through you, I think. She was so young when she died and was the foundation of your family and it was such an indelible loss for you. So knowing what she did, I'm disappointed in her. I feel robbed of the idea of her that I thought was true. I'm disappointed all of you were robbed of that, too. But I know that's not really my battle to fight."

"Have you asked your dad about any of it?" says Carolyn. "I'm not sure I want to hear any of it but I'm curious if you have."

"Not yet," Julia says. "I haven't had a chance to be alone with him and I don't know if he'll even want to talk about it, but I am going to ask."

"He's the only one now who knows what happened," Carolyn says. "I think I'd like to know too. Maybe."

"I'll figure out how lightly I'll have to tread," says Julia. "And who knows, maybe he's waited a long time to unburden himself and tell his side of the story. What a strange thing to contemplate talking about to your parent."

27

For Hutch to find out about Anne after all this time with something as simple as a test that you drop in the mail, but no revelation from Joan directly all those years, remains shocking even weeks later. He can't imagine when it will no longer be. The genetic disclosure reminds Hutch of an uneventful high school biology experiment overseen by the same teacher for years, except for the one time when it goes terribly wrong and results in explosions that blow up in students' faces, causing disfiguring burns and leading to lawsuits.

Joan hardly left a clean slate at the end of her life, and Hutch has to wonder why only tell Peter Herring half the story? Did she not know Hutch was Anne's father or did she not want to disrupt Hutch's life from beyond the grave? Or was it about not disrupting her own family? He wonders if she knew about Mark. Graham told Hutch the cancer had spread to her brain, so was her decision to tell Peter Herring about Hutch, and how to find him, influenced by her compromised cognitive function? Or was she completely clear-headed?

In the months after Mark died, as he tried to recover his footing, when he was least expecting it, Hutch would experience a moment, literally the merest fraction of a second, when he would forget Mark was gone. When he was watching a riveting Saturday afternoon baseball game that summer and would grab a beer from the fridge, unconsciously—temporarily—he would think, *I'll grab one for Mark,* even though he'd been sitting in front of the television alone for five innings.

Or, one of the cruelest, strangest reminders, when the gas gauge was practically on empty he'd think, *Goddamn it, Mark, how many times do I have to tell you to put in a couple buck's worth when you use the car?* The fact the car needed gas at all was evidence of how much Hutch was still out of his head; neither he nor Alice were driving very much so when the car ran out of gas just as he was pulling into the station to fill it on the day he realized how dangerously low it was and needed the attendant's help to push it to the pump, he felt duped by a trick being played on him by an adversary he couldn't see.

Hutch experiences the truth about Anne the same way. He'll be distracted, invested in something mundane, getting salmon from the seafood counter at New Seasons, and while he waits for it to be wrapped after he orders it, be freshly struck that she is his and Joan's child.

He is grateful for how Alice is handling it. She's never said a single word, but he believes she has to be disappointed in him that he wasn't careful during his relationship with Joan; that he didn't take the very precautions men in his situation need to in order to avoid being in some version of the situation he's in now, that they're all in. He's ashamed to admit that he had never thought about it, and he never brought it up with Joan. He assumed she was so far ahead of him in that department—she had a child already and was married—so it never occurred to him that she wasn't taking preventive measures of some kind on her end.

When he remembers how he idolized her and fantasized about the value of what they had, how heartbroken and gutted he'd felt after it was over even though it was his decision, he also faces the truth that they didn't know each other very well at all. The fact that they never even discussed birth control was a perfect example that their intimacy was reckless and immature. They had never even spent the night together sleeping in the same bed.

Given that he's prone to, he has to stop himself from going down a bottomless rabbit hole about Anne's conception. At the time was Joan's marriage so troubling that she purposely got pregnant in order to have some terrible, hurtful secret in reserve but one that she never used? Despite how deeply in love Hutch was with her, it didn't grant him the ability to know her well or understand her motivations and choices.

Because Anne's looks so closely favor Joan's, and Julia looks more like Alice than she does Hutch, nothing about their appearances screams that they're related, but when they're together, as they recently have been with Hutch and Alice, it's easy to guess that they are, from, more than anything, how they carry themselves. They are roughly the same build and height, but Anne's complexion and eye color are Hutch's—more olive and dark brown—like Mark's had been, while Julia is fairer. But the one undeniable thing the girls do share, though you have to look for it, is their hands. Like Hutch, they both have long, slender square fingers; they're Hutch's mother's hands, and on a woman they're attractive in a different way than they are on a man.

He remembers minutes after Julia was born and they were marveling at her, Alice had said, "Hutch, look, she's got your fingers!"

He's sentimental, cynical, critical and angry at Joan, but he has difficulty feeling any emotion about Anne beyond gratitude for how well their meeting went, although this is another thing he imagines sharing with Mark, even after all these years. *I sure made a mess of things, so be glad you always wore a condom, son.*

But what if a woman who had had Mark's baby came out of the woodwork and dropped into their lives one day? Jesus Christ, he can't go there. The goddamn rabbit hole.

Anne already has a family, and a father. And Hutch already has a family. It's not like when divorce forces a formerly married couple and their kids to decide where and with whom they're going to spend the holidays. This is a different thing entirely. If Anne and Julia want to become close in their own right, creating a unique triangle out of Julia's friendship with Carolyn, that's up to them. Although for reasons Hutch doesn't understand, things between Julia and Carolyn have recently been rocky. And if Alice and Anne want to form some kind of alliance, he knows there's nothing he can or should do to either promote it or discourage it.

At best he's unnecessary, and at worst he's unwelcome for them to find their way toward something either or both of them want. And if Anne wants anything from him, he'll do whatever he can to give her what she asks for or needs, but he's a follower with her, something he genuinely believes, and which was important for him to tell her. He is not at the helm as far as Anne goes. At the end of their lunch, she said she would be in touch. He's trying to avoid the rabbit hole of counting the days.

Hutch is a grown man; he's an old man who's getting older, but he hasn't forgotten what it felt like when he was twenty-three years old, to overlook Graham, to ignore Graham, to compete with Graham. Only recently has he had to deal with Graham. Their meeting was a necessity. And Hutch was grateful for Graham's graciousness, his aplomb. Hutch imagines himself in Graham's place and doubts he would have had the same generosity and composure that

Graham possessed, and granted him what Hutch interpreted rightly or not, as unspoken forgiveness.

He and Alice had pared down so much from the house in New Canaan before the move to Portland and Alice had overseen all the aspects of downsizing: the moving sale, the countless carloads of Goodwill donations, and shipping the furniture they weren't ready to part with to Julia for her to store. She wasn't sure she wanted it either, but Alice and Hutch wouldn't have room for it in the apartment, so she agreed to keep it until they could deal with it later when they had more time.

Days after Graham's visit, Alice is at Julia's to finally go through their furniture and make a decision about what to do with it, as well as determine anything else Julia wants to get rid of, and that's only part of it. Alice is on a new kick she wants to share with Julia: the KonMari Method. It's all Alice has been able to talk about since Marie Kondo's book came out a few months ago, even though at this point there is very little in their Indigo apartment that isn't essential.

"Oh, my God, Hutch," Alice said one night when she was reading the book in bed. "Can I tell you how much I wish I'd had this years ago? It would have made selling the house so much less painful. I could have been living this way for years even before we moved. This woman is a genius, truly."

And without Alice knowing, Hutch picked it up to see what all the fuss was about.

With Alice at Julia's for the afternoon tidying, organizing and deciding what to keep and throw away—going full Kondo on Jack and Julia's house—Hutch goes to the closet and takes out his drawings of Joan and when he looks at the images now, he hears Alice reading out loud from the book.

"I just love this, Hutch. Listen to what she says, *Look at each object and ask yourself, does this spark joy?*" These were the same words he read when he skimmed the thing himself.

Looking at the images of Joan, she looks exactly as he remembers her, and he can recall the afternoons he sketched them, but another part of him feels like he's come across soft, buttery sheets of paper bearing the likeness of a beautiful woman while browsing the tables at a stranger's yard sale. He has as much use for them now as he would the stranger's.

He asks himself: *Do they bring you joy?*

No. They do not. Had they ever? But now they most certainly only bring sorrow and loss and resentment and serve as a reminder of a secret he should have known; one that Anne should have known.

There is a partially full paper bag of recyclables under the sink containing signs of their lives: yogurt containers, tuna cans, flattened cereal and pasta boxes, which Hutch grabs and shoves the drawings of Joan into. The bag isn't big enough for all of them, so he gets a second one for the rest of the drawings and puts the letter from Peter Herring on top of the drawings and pushes the whole mess down into the second bag.

He grabs his keys, leaves the apartment and takes the bags to the garbage room at the end of the hall on their floor and opens the big blue recycling bin the tenants all use and which is emptied regularly. It's mostly empty, maybe just another tenant's stuff in there, and he drops the drawings of Joan and then his own recycling on top of the drawings. There's no way to know how much longer it will all be in the bin until it's emptied; the drawings could be sitting there for days while he fights the urge to change his mind as other tenants add their recycling, filling the bin.

He lays the bin on its side and pulls out his bag of recycling, all the drawings of Joan and Peter Herring's letter. He rights the bin and drops his recycling back in it again. He takes the drawings and letter, returns to the apartment and puts everything in a plastic garbage bag he pulls out from under the sink and ties it closed. He returns to the garbage room and flings the bag into the chute that leads to the bowels of the building and goes back to the apartment.

There is no additional mystery to solve and nothing to debate or decide. With Alice's help, Hutch will keep an open mind about Anne, figure out what to do or say when the need arises, but he is finished, again, with Joan. *Although we'll always have that baby between us, won't we? Proof.* And he is newly, but finally, finished with Graham.

28

Three months after Joan was diagnosed, on New Year's Day 1986, Graham and Joan were invited to an evening open house in New Canaan hosted by a younger attorney in Graham's firm who had recently been promoted and his wife. Joan had recovered from the mastectomy and had just started chemo, but hadn't yet had reconstruction and was reluctant to go.

"Can't we skip it?" she asked. Most days she was feeling and looking good, and her prognosis and the future seemed so optimistic that Graham couldn't understand her hesitancy. Joan always effortlessly outshone him at a party and Graham didn't mind.

"I want a night out with you," he said. "You deserve it. We deserve it. People have been asking about you and we have both earned some fun."

"Graham, I don't want to play the cancer card," Joan said. "And there's no way around it. It would be, *I* would be, the elephant in the room. It will be an obstacle course of a bunch of people trying to not get overheard whispering to each other, 'Look there's Joan.' I know I'm not the center of the universe Graham, but I do know people know what's going on with me and I don't want to fuel the gossip. Isn't that enough reason for you to understand why I don't want to go?"

"Yes," he said. "It absolutely is, and darling, I get it, but I'm going to push back a little and say to hell with the cancer. We'll talk about anything else but, I'll make sure of it." Graham took her hand in his. "You'll know so many people there and you know they love you, don't you? So you should expect that they will be delighted to spend some time with you. Please, Joan. We can leave whenever you want. Let's celebrate the start of a new year."

Joan had finally agreed to go, and Graham had felt right to convince her. She was buoyed by seeing so many of Graham's colleagues and their spouses, friends they'd both known for years, and no one said a word about cancer.

But after they had been there for an hour, a woman neither of them knew, a neighbor of the host, said to the group they were standing with, "I saw Alice Hutchinson the other day in the market. I can't imagine that woman's agony. Has anyone else seen or spoken to her?"

Joan had asked him to please get her another glass of wine, she was going to go and sit down. He brought back a glass for each of them and sat with her on the stairs leading to the second floor of a house they'd never been to and would never be again and after fifteen minutes Joan told him she was suddenly so tired and asked could they please leave? She was so sorry, but could they please go?

He remembered young, beautiful Joan Hamilton, and their first meeting—in his mind it was last week, yesterday, only hours ago, they were playing hearts with Richie and Judy in a bar after winning a hockey game—before their lives together began.

But no, that January 1st it was three grown daughters later, and the shared decades between them during which they loved each other and bore witness and soldiered through everything that had gotten them to this night when Joan was sick and needed Graham to take care of her at a party in New Canaan that he forced her to attend.

When he was feeling optimistic and hopeful and Joan was having a good day, Graham was convinced that the end of her life was unlived decades away, something he could keep at bay with bargaining and prayer and the fact that because of medical advancements, millions of women survived breast cancer every year. When he was worried and panicked and terrified that the light of her life was flickering and dimming by the hour and her time was winding down too fast, he knew the best medical predictions often failed, and luck and fate could neither be measured nor relied upon.

He was in control of nothing.

What a mystery she was to him. Was he to her? No, not ever. Their whole lives he was as simple and two dimensional as a photograph. He was smart, and a good provider, and he loved her, deeply, but he was no mystery to her. But she truly had been, and he had been content to coexist with that mystery.

★ ★ ★

Three days before Joan died, they'd been alone in their bedroom, and Graham was sitting in the chair next to the bed. It was early evening and Carolyn and Anne had both gone out. Joan was still lucid, although that was the last day she would be conscious. That night it was just the two of them together, privately, for the last time.

"I'm tired, Graham," she said. Her speech was sluggish. "It takes on a whole new meaning at this point. I don't even have enough energy to laugh."

"What do you mean?" Graham said. "Are you in pain?"

"No," Joan said, groggy. "I'm just so tired. I think of all the times in our lives when we complained about being tired, you know? When the girls were little or when we were jet lagged or we'd been out late at a party. Or just because it was a Thursday, when people asked, 'How are you?' And it was always convenient and pretty much always true to say, 'Oh, fine, but I'm tired.' I think back to those times and it makes me laugh. That was nothing compared to how tired I am right now."

"I'm so sorry," said Graham. "I really am." His voice grew thick and a lump in his throat started to form. "I wish there was something I could do."

"You know how much I love you, don't you?" She said, "I really hope you do." She reached out her right hand and he folded it between both of his.

"Of course," he said. "I love you, too, darling."

"Well, there was that bad time," she said. "We went through a bad time and if you ever think about it, if you've ever thought about it, I don't want you to think, or doubt how much I loved you."

"Everyone has rough times in their marriages, it's not something you should be worrying about. We've come through a lot, together."

"I know we have," said Joan. "It was just an extraordinarily bad time, that's all. And I'm sorry about it. I just wanted you to know I'm sorry. Please forgive me."

"I don't know what you're talking about," said Graham. "You have nothing to be sorry for."

He stood up from the chair and got into the bed with her, curling his body around hers. He pulled up the comforter so it covered both of them. He stroked her hair until she fell asleep. Finally, after he heard Anne and Carolyn come home, he slept too.

That night she left them for the in-between place where she was for the next three days. She called out to her sisters who were alive, and to her parents who were not, with whatever unfinished business she thought she still had to resolve. Twice toward the very end she muttered a word that sounded like "much" or "hunch," but her speech was so slurred by then, Graham didn't know what to make of it.

Graham called Ceci and told her it was time to come and stay till the end. He called Joan's sisters. Hospice arrived. Joan's group of closest friends gathered around her bed for one last visit and said goodbye.

So now, all these years later, this was the truth of his family. That night she was asking for carte blanche for something he never would have believed. And calling out for Hutch. And what Graham couldn't quite get over—it would hit him anew at random times, getting his hair cut, going to the bank, taking out the trash, waiting for the elevator—was that it was only news to them all now, but it had been true for decades. For Anne's whole life. For Graham and Joan's entire marriage.

When he thinks about the cold hard fact, *I am not Anne's father*, it feels like she has died. Although she hasn't, now Anne is gone from him in a way that was sudden and shocking, unexpected and painful. So much like a death. And equally true is this fact: Anne is his favorite. She always has been.

He doesn't think she knows, or that Joan ever had. Parents can't have favorites and can't confess if they do. Certainly he and Carolyn had a unique closeness during the last months of Joan's life when she moved home for longer than Anne had, that couldn't be duplicated by his relationship with the other two girls. The circumstances of his daughters' lives at the time—such as they were—put Carolyn in the natural position of being more of a primary co-caretaker with him. And they became so much closer because of the experience, and he loved her deeply for her sacrifice and also for the transformation he saw her make during that time, really, from a girl into a woman. She was not the same person she'd been when she moved home that she was when she returned to college.

But Anne has always amazed him. She favored Joan more than her sisters, who both looked like him, maybe that was part of it. People always said, Ceci and Carolyn were "your father's daughters." But Anne looked like her mother more than the other two and she had the same fiery ability to confront whatever she encountered as Joan did. She was independent and thrived living abroad, which Joan had never been able to do. As she grew up, Graham often felt like he must have been looking at the stages of Joan growing up, channeled through their daughter. So this is what she looked like as a toddler, teenager and adolescent, young woman. When Anne went to college, she looked very much like her mother had when she and Graham had met, and there were baby pictures of Joan and Anne that were almost indistinguishable.

Graham has been arguing with Joan in his head non-stop since he's found out, waiting in line at the deli for a sandwich, going for a run, paying the cashier at D'Agostino's. The exchange is always the same.

Why Joan? Why?

Graham. You know why. We were so young, and you were more married to law school and that world more than you were to me. You came home to sleep but little more than that.

You could have talked to me, Joan. I could have made changes. I would have. I'm not a mind reader.

Correct. A mind reader is one thing you are not.

Graham imagines her smiling at him, tilting her head, knowing what he's imagining now, is not something he would have said or done back then, and is complete bullshit. But of course, there's no way to know. It's the stuff of madness. He hasn't had her for, and has missed her for, twenty-five years. And, Graham knows, since he is the only one in command of both sides of this imaginary conversation, Joan's side is a completely subjective reflection of Graham's side of the story, what he remembers of their time, that time, them.

And he tries harder, to invite the spirit, the energy, the presence of Joan to get a more realistic side of the story. Every story has two sides, what was hers? And if it's more painful, what does it matter? It's so far in the past, Joan is dead and anything he can come up with isn't a real answer, or a newly unearthed fact, it's only him speculating. And honestly, his imaginings can't be more painful than the truth about Anne.

You say now that I could have talked to you but really, Graham. I gave so many signs that you didn't see, didn't read. If you look back now, I'm sure you'll remember one or two. That helped me decide to keep my mouth shut. I had a baby to worry about and focus on.

And then you had Hutch to focus on, too. Did you love him?

What does it matter Graham? I didn't leave you. I stayed.

I still want to know. Did you love him?

Yes. I did.

But not enough to leave me? Why didn't you?

Because I loved you, too. Because I loved you both. Because I didn't love him enough to leave you. Because it had been a mistake. I made a mistake.

But what if Graham pressed her and got angry? Raised his voice?

Goddamn it, Joan! Tell me the truth. There's no point in lying any more, not now.

I felt trapped. And I couldn't afford to leave. If you must know I stayed because of the money. I stayed because of stigma. I stayed because you were the better bet.

So our whole lives together, our entire marriage, was a lie? Wasn't based on love and partnership and the vows, for better or worse, for richer or poorer in sickness and in health? You were the one who got sick Joan, and I was there through it all, and the grief after you died, you don't know it, you can't know it. It undid me, it leveled me. Left a wound that won't ever completely heal but has just gotten smaller over time. I've never remarried and have never wanted to. I've had our girls, that has been my reward. But now this.

He imagines pouring his heart out, sobbing in all his vulnerability to try and extract from her an affirmation of her devotion to undo her infidelity that produced her second child, but not his. He continues to try and mine the possibilities of honesty, painful as they may be, that she would reveal.

If you had waited, and proposed later than you did, he imagines Joan saying, *I would have said no. I wanted to travel, and see the world, and we did. We did. As a family. I wanted more Graham, so much more, before I married and started a family. I wanted adventure and independence. I wanted to be different versions of myself before I settled on one. And I didn't know I wanted all that until it was too late. That's all. I told you I was sorry.*

There's nothing more he can do but surrender to a ghost and his imagined, hopeless, scripted conversations with her. He hopes Carolyn can mend things with Julia—surely a strong basis for their close friendship had to be that Julia reminded Carolyn of Anne—and he hopes he can be open to accepting how much Anne may want to do with Julia, Hutch and Alice. And while he can't blame her if she wants to establish a connection with them, and will support her, he doesn't want anything to do with the three of them.

Maybe he will ask Carolyn what she thinks of him seeing a therapist. He will ask objectively, knowing that her answer can only be subjective, and with her light and loving touch might rely on comedy. Tragedy plus time.

Good one Dad, she might say, and then follow up with a joke. *When the traumatized father asked his daughter the therapist if he should start therapy, what did she say?*

I don't know Carolyn, what did she say?

I'd like to hear what you think.

Celeste, Margaret, Bridget and Jacqueline are all still alive—did Joan ever tell any of them? Graham can't imagine she would have, but what does he know, sisters have their own allegiances and alienations, certainly his daughters—*goddamn it, they are* all *my daughters!* —do and have, their whole lives. And he can't imagine asking any of them or sharing this new revelation. At the core of his pain, there is an unwavering kernel of protectiveness of Joan, like a reflex, that even now he will loyally maintain.

And why in the world did someone invent this goddamn 23andMe Pandora's box in the first place? It's like a loaded gun everyone knows not to touch. In the wrong hands, accidentally handled or mistaken for being empty of bullets, you get a fatal outcome no one can undo. The only recourse left is to ask, Why? To play the game of What If. To blame someone else for knowing, or not knowing what you did, and didn't think to mention.

He will start seeing a therapist who will ask him to examine his life, choices and feelings, what he knows, what and how he's lived, things he can't change and how to accept them, and like a mantra, he'll come back to the same thought again and again and again until one day he realizes he hasn't thought about it:

We had a wonderful life and a wonderful marriage and three wonderful daughters. I loved her fiercely. Fuck 23andMe. If I knew then what I know now and had the chance to do it all over again, I would. She made a mistake. I forgive her.

Any relationship Anne has with Hutch and his family doesn't dictate that Graham must also have one, or even suggests that he should. Anne might be Hutch's daughter, but Graham is her father. And, when he thinks about Hutch, who loved Joan, too, and who always, from the beginning, knew about Graham—who was perpetually between them and in the way—he puts himself in the other man's shoes. He imagines Hutch wouldn't want Graham in his life any more than Graham would want to be there. That bitter sentiment is the one final thing they'll share, the very last thing they'll ever have in common.

NEW YORK

AUGUST 1988

29

Even without a calendar, the telltale signs of late summer are obvious. It's not only the later sunrises and earlier sunsets. There's a shift in how the air smells, and the sunlight has a different slant to it during the day. The clues that fall, Halloween, the darker, shorter days and holiday seasons are right around the corner. I'm not wistful about any other seasonal transitions the way I am about this one. Maybe because summer and fall are my favorites. Maybe it's because they are the two most significant; summer marks the end of one school year, and fall brings the beginning of a new one. And for so many years, my life, my family's lives, revolved around those cycles.

But those years are behind us, and now the empty nest looms for Graham and me. It's true what they say—the days are long, but the years are short. I'm not ready. I wish we'd had six children so three of them would still be home with us. Carolyn starts her freshman year at Amherst next week and has been in her own world cleaning out closets and drawers, bagging what she wants to give away and packing what she wants to take. Although I've offered, she says she doesn't need my help but says she'll ask if she does. At least she lets me sit in her room with a book anyway and watch her.

While she packs, she listens to CDs: Tracy Chapman and The Cure and U2, and sings along with the lyrics. In these last few days before she leaves, I'm inventing things to talk about, finding ways to squeeze value out of our conversations, no matter how trivial. I ask Carolyn the names of the bands and songs and she tells me. I like "Fast Car," and most of the songs on *The Joshua Tree*.

When Carolyn concentrates—so focused on packing—she has the same deep, single crease between her eyebrows that Graham and Ceci have too—a shared trait we call The Cavanaugh Trench. In more than one photo, when Graham, Ceci and Carolyn are squinting at the sun, their expressions are identical.

I try and memorize the feeling of her so I can recall it after we get home from dropping her off. Graham and I will stop in Boston for a night or two and see Ceci, John and Wyatt. The baby is six months old now, such a delightful age, and holding him is a lovely reminder of how my own babies felt. Such a long time ago. Once we're back, I'll write my weekly letter to Anne. She's been living in Italy for over a year now and although she came home for Christmas last year, I worry that as more time goes by, the flimsy air mail stationery we use to share our news across thousands of miles will be the only thing connecting us.

How I'm not looking forward to a quiet, empty apartment! I've mostly wept quietly, but a few times openly to Graham, and although he doesn't feel the same strange grief of missing our daughters now that they're out in the world, or at least as deeply, he understands why it feels like a loss to me. They have been my whole life. My greatest treasures.

The good news is that I'm feeling optimistic about remission and the success of the chemotherapy and radiation. Time will tell, but now that will be my focus—being cancer-free. Carolyn will be home for Thanksgiving, and Christmas not long after. And, if Anne's trips home become less frequent, we will go see her. What a wonderful plan to look forward to, Christmas in Italy!

Yet I'm painfully aware of the old adage: You want to make God laugh, tell Him your plans. But what's the joy of life without things to look forward to? None of us knows what's going to happen, but planning is evidence of hope and faith at work. It's human nature. It makes us feel free. It's what will get me through the coming months until the next time my family is home, and together again.

Photo: Jamie Bosworth Photography

ABOUT THE AUTHOR

POLLY DUGAN is the author of the linked story collection, *So Much a Part of You*, and the novel, *The Sweetheart Deal*. Her short fiction has appeared in *Narrative* and *Line Zero*. She is a contributing author to *Before and After the Book Deal: A Writer's Guide to Finishing, Publishing, Promoting, and Surviving Your First Book* by Courtney Maum. She is a graduate of Dickinson College and the Denver Publishing Institute, a former employee of Powell's Books and Guide Dogs for the Blind, a Tin House Summer Workshop alum and a former submissions reader for *Tin House* magazine. She lives in Portland and Manzanita, Oregon with her family.

ACKNOWLEDGMENTS

I began this novel in late 2014, and for most of a decade completing it felt like a Sisyphean task. Thank you to Vicki DeArmon, Julia Park Tracey, Suzy Vitello and the entire team at Sibylline Press for giving this book a home, getting it out into the world and into the hands of its readers. Special thanks to Alicia Feltman for the exquisite cover design. I'm honored to be included in the community of Sibyl Sisters.

Many thanks to Emily Chenoweth and Michelle Wildgen, who provided feedback on multiple drafts over the years as I continued to try and craft this story into the book I believed it could be. In 2015, Emily's class Writing a Novel in Eight Weeks, through Literary Arts, one of the pillars of Portland, Oregon's writing community, was the first time I got input from other writers and learned maybe I should stick with it. During the pandemic Emily's virtual classes offered prompts that sections of this book are literally the product of; without her prompts, chapters of this book simply would not exist.

The character of Joan Cavanaugh has been with me for a very long time, since August of 2010, when I returned to working as an instructor at Guide Dogs for the Blind and dedicated my lunch breaks to writing. The story, "Legacies," which appears in my linked collection, *So Much a Part of You*, introduces Joan, and was the result of those lunch break writing sessions. This was also the story I workshopped with

Steve Almond at the Tin House Summer Workshop in July 2011, from which I got invaluable feedback, from both Steve and my workshop peers. The idea for this book arose from the potential at the conclusion of "Legacies;" more than one reader asked me if the main character in that story honored Joan's dying wish. As I delved into exploring that question, I recognized there was much more to Joan and her life. I only had to stay in the chair and figure out what that was. This book is very much her story.

Although she is a fictional character, Joan is a composite of three people who inspired her development: my dear friend Joan Weber, my beloved aunt, Maria Levinson, and my extraordinary mother, Judy Sweeny. These women lived adventurous, accomplished, passionate lives, and along with countless others, I loved them. They are dearly missed.

As I was working on this book and periodically talked about the project, I was struck by how many people knew families in similar circumstances. I had already begun working on this novel when I read Dani Shapiro's wonderful memoir, *Inheritance*, and understood what unforeseen DNA revelations of 23andMe.com and Ancestry.com often elicit: shock, betrayal, and an existential unmooring when people learn what they have believed all their lives is ultimately fiction. I cannot begin to know what ensues for families going through these painful experiences or how complicated those discoveries and their aftermaths are. I hope this book has captured how I imagined this complex dynamic with authenticity and compassion.

With the help of a friend's family, I was able to research and create what would have been Anne's 23andMe results with as much accuracy as possible. Any mistakes are my own.

I am beyond grateful to my writer and non-writer friends: Steve Almond, Jodi Angel, Emily Chenoweth, Elise Juska,

Edan Lepucki, Scott Nadelson, Susan Perabo, Laura Sims, Carolyn Allison, Brooke Noli and Weezy Seward. You have all supported this book, in one way or another, and some of you have inspired details that have made their way to these pages. To those friends: Thank you for always sharing your stories and experiences with me knowing they may show up in my work.

Patrick: my champion, my best time, my everything, the very best husband and father. Thank you for always believing in everything I have ever wanted to pursue and helping to make it possible. Thank you for our boys.

Finn and Brady: this one's for you. Being your mother has been the greatest joy, gift and 'work' of my life. I am the richest woman in the world for knowing the extraordinary humans you have become, and are still becoming. You know the rest: I love you a ton and a half million, and more than the world.

STUDY GUIDE QUESTIONS

1. Do you know anyone with a 23andMe.com or Ancestry.com story that revealed unexpected paternity/maternity/siblings or other previously unknown close relatives? Do you know someone who has any long-held family secret/s that came out at some point because of a specific event: a surprise guest at a reunion or a deathbed confession?

2. Have you experienced significant events with people in your life that coincide with other events to make you marvel at the coincidence/serendipity/synchronicity at work in the world? One writer has stated that coincidence works in fiction only if it makes a character's life worse, not better. Have any 'coincidences' you've had made your life better, worse, neither or both?

3. If you have formed deep, new friendships as an adult, what have been the factors that have bound you so closely? Julia and Carolyn's friendship has the foundation of shared grief, which they build upon after their initial connection. How do the factors that bind you in these friendships later in life differ from ways you connected with a dear friend as a child, teen, or young adult?

4. How do you feel about Joan and her decision? Do you stand in moral judgement of her choice? Do you have

compassion or empathy for her? Can you understand why she made the choice she did? If you can, try to imagine what you would have done in her place during that time. Do you pass any moral judgment on Graham or Hutch and their behaviors?

5. Hutch and Graham imbibe and talk at a bar while stuck in an airport. Have you ever—with or without drinking—connected in a meaningful way with a stranger on a plane or in an airport bar? If so, did you exchange names and any other information, or not?

6. At any time while you were growing up, did you ever feel disconnected and like you didn't belong in your family of origin? Did you ever imagine being a member of another family? If so, why and who was the family or families?

7. It's not uncommon for someone who has lived a perceived 'good life' to be put on a pedestal or 'canonized' in a way after they have died by their loved ones. Have you experienced a situation or know someone who did so with a family member only to be disappointed by the discovery of who they truly were, or something they did that came to light after they passed away? Alternately, have you ever learned something redeeming about someone who was difficult to deal with in life after they died?

8. Do you know any parents of adult children, with their own families, who have relocated to be close to them? What has that transition been like?

9. Did anything in the book surprise you? Why?

Sibylline Press is proud to publish the brilliant work of women authors over 50. We are a woman-owned publishing company and, like our authors, represent women of a certain age.

ALSO AVAILABLE FROM
Sibylline Press

Other People's Kids: A Novel
By Kim Culbertson
FICTION
392 pages, Trade Paper, $22
ISBN: 9781960573438
Also available as an ebook AND AUDIOBOOK

After a violent incident at her prestigious Bay Area school, English teacher Chelsea Garden returns to her rural hometown seeking refuge and a fresh start. There, she reconnects with a burned-out principal and an old flame, both working at the local high school. *Other People's Kids* follows three educators at different stages of their careers as they navigate second chances, personal crossroads, and the risks of starting over.

Collateral Stardust: Chasing Warren Beatty and Other Foolish Things
By Nikki Nash
MEMOIR
280 pages, Trade Paper, $19
ISBN: 9781960573421
Also available as an ebook AND AUDIOBOOK

Raised in a chaotic, bohemian Hollywood household, teenage Nikki Nash becomes fixated on a bold mission: meet and win over Warren Beatty. With determination and a detailed plan, at eighteen, working in a restaurant near the Beverly Wilshire, her long-shot dream collides with reality. While Warren remains ever present in her life, this is really the story of one woman navigating Hollywood as a producer, comedian, and actor in the eccentric fringes of L.A., brushing up against fame, danger, and dysfunction.

Seeds of the Pomegranate: A Novel
By Suzanne Samuels

HISTORICAL FICTION
416 pages, Trade Paper, $22
ISBN: 9781960573445
Also available as an ebook and audiobook

After illness derails her dreams of becoming a painter in Sicily, Mimi Inglese immigrates to New York, only to be dragged into her father's criminal underworld. When he's imprisoned, she turns to counterfeiting to survive, using her artistic gift to forge a path through Gangland chaos. As violence closes in, Mimi must risk everything to escape a life built on desperation and reclaim the future she once imagined.

You Could Be Happy Here: A Novel
By Erin Van Rheenen

FICTION
280 pages, Trade Paper, $19
ISBN: 9781960573476
Also available as an ebook and audiobook

When Lucy loses her mother and discovers her real father may be a man from her childhood summers in Costa Rica, she sets out to find him—and herself. But the village she returns to is no longer the paradise she remembers, and her search raises more questions than answers. *You Could be Happy Here* is a story of identity, belonging, and redefining home in a world that no longer fits the past.

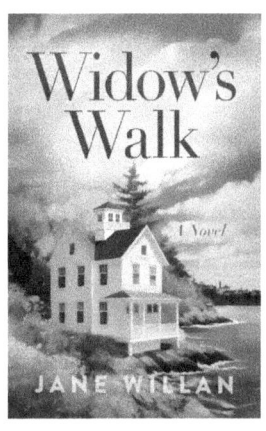

Widow's Walk: A Novel
By Jane Willan

FICTION
336 pages, Trade Paper, $20
ISBN: 9781960573452
Also available as an ebook and audiobook

When new Reverend Miranda McCurdy brings progressive change to a tradition-bound coastal church in Maine, her efforts spark fierce resistance—especially after she challenges the town's beloved Thanksgiving pageant. As the congregation splinters and a woman seeking sanctuary raises the stakes, Miranda must choose between fleeing back to her old life or staying to fight for the community she's slowly come to love. A stray dog and a mysterious stranger may tip the scales in this story of conviction, belonging, and second chances.

Reviving Artemis: The Making of a Huntress
By Deborah Lee Luskin

MEMOIR
280 pages, Trade Paper, $19
ISBN: 9781960573759
Also available as an ebook and audiobook

At sixty, longtime writer, gardener, and teacher Luskin feels a wild new calling: to leave the safety of her garden and learn to hunt deer. *Reviving Artemis* follows her late-in-life transformation as she confronts fear, embraces the forest, and reclaims a primal connection to nature. Blending humor, vulnerability, and myth, it's the story of a woman choosing to age on her own fierce terms.

 For more books from **Sibylline Press**, please visit our website at **sibyllinepress.com**

www.ingramcontent.com/pod-product-compliance
Lightning Source LLC
Jackson TN
JSHW021152230925
91464JS00005BA/39